Lost On Route 66

Tales from the Mother Road

Edited by
Katelyn Bohl and
Eric Wilder

With a foreword by
r. r. bryan

No part of this book may be reproduced or utilized in any form or by any means: electronic, mechanical or otherwise, including photocopying, recording or by any informational storage and retrieval system without permission in writing from the copyright owner.

Copyright © 2010 by Gondwana Press LLC

FIRST EDITION

Cover photo by Katelyn Bohl

ISBN: 978-0-9791165-1-3

Published by Gondwana Press LLC
Edmond, Oklahoma
www.GondwanaPress.com

For everyone that has found solace and inspiration along the Mother Road.

Table of Contents

6	r. r. bryan	Foreword

Fiction

8	Russell D. Walker	Only on Route 66
13	Bo Drury	One Summer on Route 66
18	Tanja Cilia	Route 66
50	Tim Bemis	End of America
100	Willy	Walter's Last Ride
128	Linda Neal Reising	Arizona Highways
148	J. Myers Birsner	The Prize

Essays

31	Jacqueline Seewald	Life's Little Lessons
36	Sue Townley-Monkress	Memories of the Road
39	James Piliero	Discovering Route 66
69	Margaret Melloy Guziak	Are There Many Trains in Gallup?
72	Elizabeth Rogge	I Got My Grapefruit on Route 66
74	Jo Gray	Old Route 66
78	G. Terry Felts	Lost on Route 66
85	Janet Galloway	Pauline's Bait and Tackle
90	Luke Black	Pop Hick's, America's Kitchen
121	Jimmy J. Pack, Jr.	Conelrad in the Wigwam

Poetry

46	Ron Roberson	66 to 99
83	Jack Horne	Hitchhiker
126	Linda Neal Reising	Homecoming

Foreword

r. r. bryan

A few years ago, Oklahoma City quietly played host to Paul McCartney and his girlfriend Nancy Shevell as they stayed over one night. Traveling without an entourage or fanfare, the couple slipped in under the cover of darkness, but was spotted at a popular Bricktown haunt while enjoying dinner. Their cover blown, Sir Paul let it be known that they were on a trek: one that would take them along storied Route 66, all the way from Illinois to the Santa Monica pier.

Such is the allure of Route 66 that even British Knights desire to see and experience it. They aren't the only ones: according to the curator of the Round Barn Museum in Arcadia, Oklahoma, rarely a day passes that it doesn't receive visitors, not just from America, but from many countries. Every day, people from all over begin their own odyssey of discovery along the old highway.

If you are intrigued by the romance of Route 66 but aren't ready just yet to head up the road in a red Corvette or a 1989 Ford Bronco, as Sir Paul drove, then read *Lost on Route 66* and take a memorable mental ride in a 1955 two-door red and white Ford Crown Vic. Join a young woman at her father's dry-dirt Oklahoma farm as she watches the procession of Okies leave for a better life in California. Listen to the mournful whistle of slow-moving trains as they traverse a rainstorm in Gallup, New Mexico. Ride an old Appaloosa on its last journey, and watch the sunset in Arizona on a majestic saguaro cactus. Feel Andy Payne's fatigue as he races across America and into the history books.

Please take my advice—hitch a ride on a dream and get lost on Route 66.

r. r. bryan

Only on Route 66

Russell D. Walker

Forest fires, start from scratch, think, before you toss that match! Burma Shave.

This is the first form of advertising I remember—small colored signs set atop many consecutive fence posts along the highway. Each sign held two, three words max. They always exhibited a sponsor on the last board. The people who placed these signs along the road must have been geniuses as the angle of each was perfect for the passerby to view. I always thought it interesting that the words seemed to stay in view longer than other billboard ads.

Farmers here love their land. Toss your junk in the can! Bardahl.

About this time, a President's wife started a campaign to clean up America's highways and to raise the country's ecological perception. During the fifties, beer cans, trash and whatever else could be thrown out the window of a moving automobile lined the highways and filled the bar ditches. One woman's actions prompted radical changes in the psyche of America.

Oklahoma had just begun a mowing program of the bar ditch expanses between the paved highway and farmer's fences, the fence line denoting the boundary of the State's maintenance responsibility. Cutting the brush and weeds on the side of the road made a dramatic difference in the appearance of the highway and surrounding lands. As a neat and tidy person, even at an early age, I felt good about it all.

When I was seven, I sat in the back seat of my dad's 1955 two-door red and white Ford Crown Victoria, gazing out the window, as telephone poles and their long black lines seemed to jump past me. Up and down, the lines raced from pole to pole. In real time, this repetitive action produced a symphony of movement that excited my young eyes and grasping mind. Depending on the speed the car was moving, the movement of the passing poles actually kept time with the AM music on the Crown Vic's radio. Oh, the observations and things that kept a young lad entertained.

I remember a road trip to my grandma's house. She lived five miles west of Sapulpa, Oklahoma, on the south side of the road, in plain view of the Mother of all roads, Route 66. The traffic passing her house every day made it seem that she lived at the crossroads of the entire world. Maybe she did.

Her house sat back from the road surrounded for protection by a double row of trees, planted at the end of the dust bowl years in an attempt at soil conservation. Yes, it was a time of growing awareness.

The trees acted as buffers against highway noise and provided cooling shade to the house and the small estate's outbuildings—Grandpa's tool shed, the chicken house and the shed where Grandpa kept his tractor. It was in Grandpa's tractor shed that I saw my first can of Bardahl oil and connected it to the sign on the side of the road. Interestingly, Bardahl was an American Oil Company founded by an immigrant from Norway.

We had left our home in Oklahoma City early that morning in order to beat the heat and cool air streamed back across my face through an open window. As we entered the lowland crop floodplains near Arcadia, the monotony of the telephone poles became trancelike and I inexplicably felt as though something was wrong.

Standing in the back seat of the car, I stared to the west through the rear window. In the reddish orange glow of morning, I saw a flickering pearl-shaped object hovering just above the horizon, its pulsating colors changing from pink to bluish white. In my young mind, I felt as though, whatever it was, it had us in its sights and was coming after us. I had no idea what it was, but I was frightened.

Not wanting to alarm Dad, I continued staring at the strange object, as if my gaze might somehow chase it away. As we topped a hill and dipped into the valley syncline ahead, it disappeared. My mind raced, wondering what I had actually seen, and what, if anything, I should tell my dad.

Continuing on, we passed a number of pecan groves and cultivated fields. From the open window, I could hear locusts, denoting that summer was in full swing. Glancing back as we topped the hill, I saw it again. This time it was even closer than before, spinning as it reflected the rays of the sun. Suddenly, the fibers in the car seats stood upright as if drawn toward the object.

"Dad, can't we go any faster?"

His reply was terse.

"We had better keep it at the speed limit."

Great, I thought. At sixty miles an hour, this thing will be on us in no time.

Though Dad had no idea why I had made the request for more speed, he never questioned it, and maybe even sped up a little. The glowing orb grew larger, like my eyes, and was now just behind us. I gripped the passenger strap and held my breath.

Around each of the highway's swerving corners the new tires on the Crown Vic seemed to scream in defiance. I had no doubt left in my mind—the object above us was definitely a space ship, its alien crewmembers intent on capturing Dad and me, or worse. Looking on the floor for something to defend myself with I found only an empty paper orange juice cup. My young mind raced, thinking, *THIS IS NOT GOOD!*

Even at sixty, I made out the words: In the sky, pink and blue, Don't cry, It'll get you—Burma Shave.

By now, the spaceship lay directly above us, just as the Crown Vic lurched to the right. Loose gravel blasted the sides of the car as its brakes locked up and a cloud of white dust engulfed us.

"Wake up Rusty. We're at Grandma's."

I opened my eyes to see Dad and a woman's warm and smiling face, her brow furrowed with lines of experience, happiness and pain. It was Grandma.

As I stepped from the car, the memory of my dream still feeling very real, I looked at my grandparent's house, and then back at the Mother Road with its seemingly endless procession of passing vehicles and Burma Shave signs.

Maybe it was only a dream, but it left an indelible memory in my mind of a time and a place when reading signs on the side of the road were all part of life's great adventure, along with the dreams they inspired.

Russell D. Walker is a writer and geologist who lives, writes and works in Oklahoma City, Oklahoma—except when he and his wonderful wife Julia are off fishing in Florida, or along the Texas Gulf Coast. He is the author of the fantasy novel *Michelle and the Magic Timepiece*.

One Summer on Route 66

Bo Drury

The bug moved slowly across the dirt, pushing and guiding the perfect ball he had created of manure gathered from the cowshed. Polly, lying on her stomach on the splintered porch of the old farmhouse watched curiously. Wisps of golden hair flew around her oval face and her brown eyes watched intently as the bug traveled over the uneven ground, his spindly legs working continuously. What was he going to do with it she wondered, where was he going? He will never get there she thought.

Losing interest, she rolled over on her back and looked past the cover of the porch to the white billowing clouds gathering on the horizon. They were in constant motion, building and ebbing, rising here and falling there, going nowhere. It was the same with her she thought, going nowhere.

She could hear the traffic on the highway across the wheat field. Highway 66, some big shot person in Oklahoma had named it, Pa said. Talk was they were gonna pave it soon. Right now, there was a constant dust cloud hovering over it caused by the powdered rock and dirt that made up the surface. It had put many folks to work busting up rock at the gravel pit to build the road. I 'spose it had been a good thing. They paid a dollar a day and that had fed a bunch of hungry folks around here. Even Pa had done it for a while but now that pit was closed down and lots of folks was out of work.

It was a busy road at night. You could see the car lights snaking across the country in the dark. Polly wondered about all those folks leaving their homes and making that long trip. Where were they all going?

A bunch of 'em got lost or caught sight of the windmill and wandered past our old farmhouse. Most had hungry kids in the car and Mama always fed 'em something. It wasn't like we had a lot to eat ourselves but Mama always found something to share. She loved kids. Pa helped with a little gas or fixing flats and filling up their canvas water bags before sending them on their way. Our old windmill sure came in handy it seemed. It was a favorite with everyone that stopped by. Every vehicle that left had a dripping bagful of water tied to the front of their radiator.

Pa said he wasn't about to leave the farm. As long as he had it, we had a place to live. He wasn't sure those folks would when they got to where they were headed.

Lost On Route 66

One of these days I'm gonna go down that road, Polly thought to herself. Maybe to Amarillo or even to New Mexico. Lots of folks that stopped by talked of going all the way to California. Now that the road was built, they said it went from one side of the world to the other. They said California was a golden opportunity, money to be made by the bucketful. She didn't know why her Pa didn't just jump at the chance. She would if she was old enough.

Clouds were building in the southwest; if it rained that old dirt road would be a muddy mess. Chances were some more folks might be stopping in; maybe even spend the night, maybe even more than that. She would be glad; it got mighty lonesome out here on this old farm in the summer. She liked to visit with all the families that laid overnight.

The county road grading crew stopped to get a drink from the well when they came by. When her Pa was around, they would sit in the shade of the big elm by the well and visit a spell. Some of them would lay in the shade and take a nap. She heard them coming down the road, moving slow, stirring up the dirt as they came. This day there was a pickup truck following them. They stopped and piled down off the grader and out of the truck to come across the yard.

"Mornin' Missy," The man from the truck spoke, "Mind if we get a drink of that good water ya'll have here?"

Polly sat up and looked them over. They had someone new with them. A boy with the bluest eyes she had ever seen. He had to be at least a head taller than she was and the dirt on his face did little to conceal his good looks.

She shook her head, not saying anything as they continued on to the barrel of water. The boy hesitated. They looked each other over. Polly felt herself blush and glanced away.

The men took down the tin cup that hung on a nail, skimmed the dirt off the water in the barrel, each drinking their fill. Sam, the grader driver took his hat off and poured a dipper of water over his head, cooling down. It was hot and dirty work. Polly watched.

The man who had spoken earlier smiled, took off his hat, and looked at Polly.

"This here's my nephew, Chip, gonna be helping Sam out this summer on the roads. Learning the trade. He will be stopping by from time to time."

Wiping the sweat from his forehead, he put his hat back on. "Thanks for the drink, Missy," he said and started for the truck.

"My name's Polly," she said, looking at the boy. He nodded and followed his uncle.

Sam wiped his face with a big red bandana and smiled at her.

"See ya next time, Polly."

Polly, her eyes following them, never moved from her spot on the porch. The boy looked back as they drove away and raised his hand in a wave unseen by the others.

Leaning back on the porch and looking up at the clouds, she smiled. Maybe it wouldn't be such a bad summer after all. Guess she would wait about traveling down Route 66 for a while.

Remembering the bug, Polly sat up and looked to see how far he had traveled. He was almost to the fence. He had gone at least three feet. He might get there after all, wherever that was.

Bo Drury, born Elizabeth Paulann Lockhart and raised in the Texas Panhandle, had the advantage of growing up in the country and developing a great love and respect for nature and the plains. She reveled in her father's tall tales and stories of her ancestors that helped tame the Wild West. From her sixth great-grandfather Daniel Boone to her paternal grandparents making the land run into Indian Territory of Oklahoma, she has many stories to tell.

With a ranching heritage on one side and a newspaper family on the other, her desire to write began at an early age after reading a story by Zane Gray. Living in Texas near her four sons, fifteen grandchildren, twenty-three goats and two worthless dogs she loves, you will find her busy 'painting' stories of the west either at her easel or on her computer. Bo has written several western short stories. You may contact her at bodrury2@sbcglobal.net.

Route 66

Tanja Cilia

"Live long and prosper!" he grinned, giving me the Nazi salute. The others laughed.

I blanched. To you, this might sound banal and baffling, but I knew where this was leading.

His combination of the words from the Vulcan salute juxtaposed with that particular signal showed that it was over between us. The other people in the room failed to recognize the irony—they thought it was just a continuation of the in-joke; he could do the rooster sign only with his left hand.

This, then, was my ultimatum. I acquiesce, or I lose my job.

What he did not know was that I was pregnant with his child—as was his wife. I realize now that I was yet miles away from becoming a hard-as-nails, award-winning journalist, or did I become the way I am because of that?

We planned what was to be my journey along Route 66 with the same meticulousness that we had plotted our trysts. We left nothing to chance; if plan A failed, there was Plan B. If they both collapsed, there was Plan C. We were king makers, sure of victory, and never considered the possibility of a Plan B, let alone Plan C.

Considering that over two hundred thousand people used this "road to opportunity" to transfer to California in search of a better future than could be offered by the Dust Bowl, there was no reason why my GPS-equipped FWD could fail.

The Lincoln made history because it was the first coast-to-coast highway. The Dixie connected the U.S. Midwest with the southern United States. Highways had names.

Route 66 was special from the start—it had a number and was never meant to follow the linear tradition; its raison d'être was to imbue the backwoods with life, and marry the Great Outside with rural communities. On paper, the label U.S. 66 meant the Chicago to Los Angeles route. Off the record, people understood that along the way, it would link the main streets of towns, cities and villages. Apart from being a magnet for tourists, the route was a boon to truckers because it bypassed the treacherous Rocky Mountain passes and followed a southern route that was passable all year round.

It is one of those strange-but-true factoids that until the completion of the transcontinental railroad in 1867, it was swifter and easier to sail a ship all the way around the southern tip of South America than to journey cross-country across uncharted deserts and other hostile terrains.

While legislation for public highways first appeared in 1916, with revisions in 1921, it was not until Congress enacted an even more comprehensive version of the act in 1925 that the government executed its plan for national highway construction.

Officially, they assigned the numerical designation 66 to the Chicago to Los Angeles route in the summer of 1926. This designation acknowledged the road as one of the nation's principal east-west arteries.

From the outset, public road planners intended U.S. 66 to connect the main streets of rural and urban communities along its course for the most practical of reasons: prior to this time, most small towns had no access to a major national thoroughfare.

None of this crossed my mind as his hands brushed mine. He avoided my eyes. There was an aura of expectation in the Features Department that day.

Someone began singing snatches of the Bobby Troup song, improvising when he did not know the words, and making a right hash of it.

"If you ever plan to motor west, tum tum way, take the highway that is best—It winds from Chicago to L.A. More than de-dinn all the way—Now you go through Saint Louis—Joplin, Missouri—and many places, blah blah, San Bernardino, yeah yeah—Amarillo and Arizona too—

Won't you get hip to this timely tip?
Du-bi-du-dah-dey—
He refused to put a sock in it until someone threw a glass of ice tea at him and he had to go wash the stickiness off.

The Mother Road, some insist, should be the mother road—lower case, one defining word for the road that made America. Cyrus Avery, the highway commissioner of Tulsa in Oklahoma, spearheaded the drive to link Chicago, Illinois and Los Angeles, California through his hometown. A neat way of putting it on the map, wouldn't you say?

It didn't work until John Woodruff of Springfield, Missouri got in on the act, and the combination of his ideas, hopes, dreams and imaginings fused with the inception of a national program of highway and road development.

In any case, the aforementioned song is merely a list of names strung together. The idea came to Troup, a former marine captain and drummer with the Tommy Dorsey Band, as he was driving west from Pennsylvania to Los Angeles.

When Interstate 40 replaced Route 66, Winona, unlike Flagstaff a few miles down the road, did not get an access ramp—and that all but killed it. In fact, not many people realize that it is where Ms. Ryder got her name, but I digress. Winona is the only town that is out of sequence—and it appears in the song mainly because it rhymes with Arizona.

Troup had said in an interview that the phrase *Get Your Kicks on Route 66* and the tune for the song had materialized from thin air, as he drove out of Harrisburg in his green 1941 Buick convertible. He caught the 66 in Chicago, getting to L.A. a fortnight later.

Hard put to come up with the lyrics, he just used the names of the places the road passed through. At least this is what a wizened farmer whose pop worked the land in the Texas Panhandle told me. I will fix it—one day, Troup said—a little late now as more than one-hundred-fifty songsters have already covered it.

My granny had jet earrings. It was fashionable to wear them when one was in mourning—earrings, a pendant and a ring. Now, I wear jet earrings. Am I in mourning? I don't know.

She left them to me in her will; I was not even born, but she said that they belonged to her first descendant born with gold-flecked, aquamarine eyes—her eyes. My twin died before we were born, but I know for sure that her eyes were a clear cornflower blue.

The luminescence of freshly poured tarmac and a faint smell of gasoline make me retch. It has a dull shine, like that of my jewelry.

I laugh away suggestions from my driver that it could be morning sickness. What does he know? By the time the baby is born, I will be back in Malta, and no one will be the wiser.

It was John Steinbeck, in *The Grapes of Wrath*, who coined the term Mother Road for Route 66. John Ford's intense black-and-white blockbuster seared these words of fire into the encyclopedias for all time.

You know how in France, Louis Napoleon reduced unemployment to zero in the Second

Empire, when he got gangs of men to dig up holes, and even more to fill them up again?

Well, from 1933 to 1938, every state contributed hundreds of unemployed youths to road gangs. This mighty workforce got the final miles of road paved. By 1938, the Press boasted, "the Chicago to Los Angeles highway is continuously paved."

I heard this from one of the fellow patrons at Comfort Inn Santa Rosa, where I stopped for the night—it is just a stone's throw away (if you can throw a stone one-hundred yards that is!) from Exit 277. I'll see how I can work it into my story, later.

That night, I had a weird experience. I attributed it to the fact that I'd been reading the collection of newspaper cuttings about the Bristow, Oklahoma Gas Station ghost, and others, given to me by the owner of the Inn himself, practically the minute they found out I worked in the Press. Is it true that ghosts have a great affinity for gas stations, movie theaters and motels?

With Route 66—when gas was still just twenty-five cents a gallon or less—there had to be service stations, and plenty of them. Different petroleum companies laid claim to the business, making sure that their logos were easily visible through the sun-and-dust haze from miles away. At first, they were just a place where you could fill up your tank and go. Later, they evolved into body shops, where you could get your vehicle serviced and buy new tries if you needed them. Some had motels and diners tagged on. Some enterprising owners went whole hog and provided pools and floor shows.

Storm White Feather, lounging on a lawn chair just outside Chas Jacob's Painted Desert Trading Post, told me this and much more. Since I wasn't feeling up to par, I didn't take notes, and this is all I can remember.

As I stepped out of the shower, it was as if the silvered lining of the glass has melted, and instead, there is was molten sheet of dark glass with ominous shadows, threatening to engulf me inside it.

Somehow, in my semi-lucid state, I knew there was a logical explanation for this—despite the fact that my hair stood on end.

* * *

In this dream—or was it a dream?—I was telling someone about when I read *Through the Looking Glass* for Book Week at my alma mater. They always invite minor celebrities like myself to attract visitors, and to instill the notion in students that they can "make it" if they try, even if they are attending an inner city school for disadvantaged children.

At one point, Alice follows the rabbit down the tunnel and that is how I felt. The baby was being born and I could hear someone pecking away at typewriter keys in the background. The hospital was Joe and Aggie's Café, and it was all chrome and patent leather, and smelled of polish. I could almost hear the baby thinking, deciding on birth in America. That way, he could be a part of the story I was writing.

This did not make sense. He was a part of it before it ever began. I remember thinking, incongruously, that only Catholic Saints "do" bi-location. Then I heard the voice of my physics teacher explaining how atoms disintegrate and siphon into black holes for delivery by Pony Express. I woke up retching, shaking, and soaked with sweat.

"Is this it?" I remember asking myself when I saw stretches of the much-touted television show Route 66. It was the same as any other highway, only wider, longer, and better surfaced.

Nothing to write home about, because this was the land where we are told to expect everything to be the new, improved, bigger and better version of what would have existed elsewhere, before and since.

Route 66, the television series was another kettle of fish. George Maharis sure could sing. In fact, he cut many pop music albums. Wasn't he a handsome hunk? Isn't it a pity that . . . ? His dark and handsome good looks were such a contrast to the insipid blonde appearance of Martin Something.

You are too young to remember the series, the original one, mind, not the follow-up, because that was pathetic, and pulled soon after first airing.

Think CHIPS with a convertible Chevrolet Corvette instead of shiny motorbikes. Think Miami Vice, Streets of San Francisco, Starsky and Hutch, Dempsey and Makepeace, the Professional. Route 66 was the best by a million miles although the characters were professional wanderers and not Boys in Blue.

Largely shot on location, the two protagonists meet sweet, savory, sour, bitter and salty characters as they drove on their long and winding open road Route 66 (where else?) beat. They took care of Life, Love, and the Universe.

The producers did not (could not?) rely on high-tech gadgetry or special effects. The actors carried the series on their broad-muscled shoulders. They took care of Peace, Justice and the American Way.

As I recall, it premiered in America just after the second debate between John F. Kennedy and Richard Nixon. Like many of the series I mentioned, it had some good cop/bad cop elements. The character of my preferred one, the jazz loving, movie buff George Maharis, was the New Yorker orphan Buzz Murdock. Martin Milner (or was it Miller, Malvern, Milford, something?) was Todd Stiles, Yale-educated and younger than Murdock.

There will always be gossip about why Maharis left the series. He said it was because of the grueling filming hours, which, considering he was recovering from two bouts of hepatitis, could have been the death of him. The studio said that he was using his health, or rather the lack of it, as an excuse to break his contract and go into films. There were other issues, too.

They threw me a farewell party. Before I left for America from Malta, to take up the exchange job as an intern, my colleagues had thrown me another—two parties, in my honor, within two months. Two goodbyes, both before I left for two worlds unknown.

"Route 66, Revisited."

How ironic.

Someone muttered "Road to Damascus" and I laughed—hollowly. He was discomfited, and he sputtered and blushed, but avoided my eyes. It was then that I knew for sure that he wanted me out of his (thick, chestnut-colored) hair, forever, and not just for the duration of the trip. Some wise guy did say that a journey of a thousand miles starts with the first step.

My 'lifetime opportunity' was just his way of killing two birds with one stone. In those days, it would not do for a rookie journalist to take her employer to court to prove paternity.

* * *

"Is this the way to Amarillo?" Oh! Amarillo, the location of the Western Crossings shopping center, and that lovely Mardel Christian and Educational shop. I remember that one for sure.

"Show me the way to San Jose!" Back then, most likely you had to grin and bear it, and remain, holding the baby. I still like mixing metaphors, yes, I do. In any case, I would never have thought to procure an abortion, not with my insular, Catholic background.

Many people associate the term "Main Street" with the 'themed land' reminiscent of a turn-of-the-century American Town, to be found inside Disney Theme Parks. Nothing could be further from the truth. Main Street is the Mother Road, is Route 66. Oh, it goes through Illinois, too. I remember traveling on it back in the fifties and thinking how unique in diversity our family and our land was.

I remember Pop getting hot under the collar because naysayers insisted that any freeway with a loop in it was not a proper highway, and that if it was not straight, it was only a hodgepodge chain of streets less than one umbrella term. Poppycock and piffle! These people would never know what patriotism was if it hit them right between the eyes, where they deserved to be hit.

There's another Main Street, though; it's the tourism agency for the United States. I find that whenever there is a bypass around a village, that village is doomed. Unless, of course, there is another kind of access, as from a river, or an airport relatively near.

I got this from Jed, whom I met at Hackberry General Store in Seligman, Arizona. He told me he could trace his lineage back to the Okies. I nearly began whistling the Merle Haggard song but now I shall have to blue-pencil the negative references to Disney, though. Maybe later!

Which is the best way, to cross the United States? It's Route 66.

The wizened Japanese ex-POW who had eloped with the Pastor's daughter spoke to me in haiku. Despite my fast shorthand, it was too arduous for me to keep up with him, so I just paraphrased what he said. He actually drew the word for triplets in Japanese; it looked like three horizontal lines, and linear drawings of a vase, and a door.

"The blessing denied us was later conceded when my wife bore triplets, the first in the family within living memory," he said. "All my eleven siblings in Japan had triplets, and I expected to follow suit. We lived in a mostly white town, and there is still is an undercurrent of racism. I guess they are used to me now. They called me "Chink" which only showed how ignorant they were."

They say each state has a Springfield. I know that even though the one in Vermont won the Simpson's Village Contest, out of the fourteen that competed for it, the original was in Ohio; it's not on Route 66, but off Route 40, which is the old National Trail that pioneers took to migrate out west.

In Ohio, please note, Route 66 cities and villages are Piqua, Houston, Newport, Fort Laramie, Minster, New Bremen, St. Mary's, Spencerville, Delphos, Ottoville, Oakwood, Defiance, Archbold and Fayette.

Oh, I am getting forgetful. I tend to remember trivia these days, like how by 1984, the entire highway was decommissioned. The important stuff eludes me, such as whether we need milk or not. You really must talk to my wife about that.

I do ramble, don't I? You really must read about Chas Jacob's Painted Desert Trading Post. It was in California, I think.

If you say you are writing a travelogue, I'll tell you to go to all the places where there are ghosts and take photos. You never know, they might show up on your shots. I hear it happens.

At the time, I had to seek out the nearest telegraph office to get my copy in for the Midweek and Weekender pullout supplements. Today, all it would take would be a few taps and clicks on my laptop. O tempora, o mores. I wouldn't go back to that time.

Tanja Cilia is an Allied Newpapers (Malta) columnist, features writer and blogger. She also freelances for print and online Media, in Malta and internationally, in Maltese and English. Contact her at tanjachilja@hotmail.com.

Life's Little Lessons

Jacqueline Seewald

They say your whole life flashes before your eyes as you face death. I didn't find that to be true. My only thought was I can't die; my father will kill me! There wasn't even time to pray. My husband and I were driving over the Chain of Rocks Bridge that crosses the mighty Mississippi River and connects Missouri to Illinois on historic Route 66. It was a hot summer day in 1967. I was enjoying the scenery flashing by us as we drove along. The Old Chain of Rocks Bridge spans one of the most scenic areas of the Mississippi River. Upon completion in 1929, it shortened travel time between St. Louis, Missouri and Edwardsville, Illinois.

After agreeing to the purchase of our first and only house, we were in a happy mood, full of dreams for our future. In fact, we were planning when we would have our first baby.

Lost On Route 66

As we were crossing the bridge, approaching the bend in the middle, a metallic object dropped off the back of a pick-up truck that was directly ahead of us. Our front tire experienced an instantaneous blowout. Luckily, my husband was at the wheel. It took all his strength to keep the car from going over the guardrail as the car veered dangerously close to taking the plunge into the water far below.

The pick-up truck did not stop, just kept right on going. We were both badly shaken. I could hardly breathe and my legs felt like rubber bands. We'd nearly been killed in the blink of an eye. It was horrifying! Also horrifying was the way other cars just whizzed by completely ignoring us.

We knew we had to change the tire, but with other automobiles hurling by us, it was downright dangerous. We needed help desperately. Over forty years ago when this incident happened, there were no handy cell phones available to call the auto club or the police. As if in answer to our prayers, someone did stop to help us and offer assistance. Was it a motorist in another automobile? Perhaps a truck driver? No, not exactly. Our guardian angel was more like a Hell's Angel. He rode a Harley and was attired totally in black leather. If I wasn't already traumatized, the sight of this stranger striding toward us would have put me in cardiac arrest.

"Need help changing that tire?" he asked in a gruff voice.

My husband, Gary, and I exchanged nervous looks.

"You want to help us?" Gary asked.

"Sure, that's why I stopped."

He then situated his bike so no one would hit our car as he helped my husband change the destroyed tire. The biker removed his dark glasses and talked to us in a quiet voice, calming us. He was the only one who stopped to lend assistance.

When he took off his leather jacket, I saw tattoos undulating on both well-muscled arms. The entire experience seemed surreal. No way could I believe this was happening. My husband and I were two conservative schoolteachers. This fellow looked more like a delinquent. And yet he was helping us.

The tire was soon changed and we were ready to be on our way. We were very grateful.

"Can I please pay you for your time and trouble?" my husband asked.

"Just help the next guy you see who needs it," the biker said. "That will be the real payment."

My husband, who always shows consideration for other people anyway, found that easy enough to do. He often goes out of his way to help others. I occasionally tease him and refer to him as "the boy scout" because he always does such things as hold doors for the elderly and for women pushing baby carriages.

Neither of us ever forgot the man who helped us on the day we nearly died. We never even learned his name, but somehow, it didn't matter in the least.

That biker didn't look like the kind of person who would stop and help total strangers, yet the fact is, he most certainly did. He went out of his way to aid us and he expected no form of personal repayment. He only hoped that we would help someone else in return.

Anytime Gary and I see someone stuck on the road and in need of help, we remember that incident on Route 66 and we do our best to lend a hand. My husband and I learned something important that day. Looks really can be deceiving. I personally learned never to judge others by appearance alone. I guess you could say, I got more than my kicks on Route 66. I got enlightenment about life as well.

Jacqueline Seewald has taught creative, expository and technical writing at the university level, as well as high school English. She also worked as an academic librarian and an educational media specialist. Eight of her books of fiction are published.

Her short stories, as well as poems, essays, reviews and articles have appeared in hundreds of diverse publications such as *The Writer, Los Angeles Times, Sasee, Tea, Affaire De Coeur, Lost Treasure, The Christian Science Monitor, Pedestal, Surreal, After Dark, The Dana Literary Society Journal, Library Journal, The Erickson Tribune and Publishers Weekly*.

Her writing also appears in many anthologies, most recently *PMS: Poison, Murder, Satisfaction, With Arms Wide Open, Your Darkest Dreamspell, Cern Zoo* and several *Chicken Soup for the Soul* publications. She was nominated for a Nebula Award for 2008. Five Star/Gale published her novel *The Inferno Collection* in hardcover and

Wheeler large print. Another novel *The Drowning Pool* was published in 2009.

Memories of the Road

Sue Townley-Monkress

It coils through mountains, meanders across rivers and deserts, through miles of both austere and beautiful America. A native Oklahoman, I believe Oklahoma is one of the best places to ride Route 66, the Mother Road. I suggest it's best done in a 1963 convertible Mustang! Can't you just feel the wind in your hair?

A pilgrimage for free-wheelers, Route 66 winds over four hundred Oklahoma miles through historic towns such as Vinita, Tulsa, then on through Oklahoma City before heading westward. Oklahoma feels like the birthplace of the Mother Road, where Highway 66 is often appropriately referred to as "The Will Rogers Highway"—a native road named for a native Oklahoma son. It is the same road that many dust bowl-era Okies traveled, searching for a better life.

Vinita is a picturesque Oklahoma town with much of the established 1871 charm remaining. Beautiful architecture, as well as classic Route 66 eateries such as Clanton's Café (famous for delicious chicken-fried steak), enamors the light-hearted traveler to stop awhile, revisit and appreciate a wonderful neon past. Just outside of Vinita is a grass-inhabited stretch of the old highway that reflects its historic significance. It proves up the theory that not everything needs "fixin' up." Viewing the original road gives the flavor of a bygone era. Travel buffs can piece together the bones of old segments and take the road less traveled.

Neglected sections of Route 66 contrast strongly with work proposed in Tulsa. In 2006, nostalgic Tulsans supported restoration of their link of the east with the west by voting a tax increase! Refurbishment on the beautiful art deco-styled 11th Street bridge such as decorative lighting reminiscent of the twenties and thirties is part of the plan to keep alive the vibrancy of the road for future generations to experience.

Just west of Sapulpa, volunteer work crews recently cleaned up the undergrowth and trees which obscured a historic bridge on Route 66. Though the route now meanders a bit to the south of the bridge, it is the only remaining brick-decked bridge on the entire route. Taking Route 66 from Tulsa to Oklahoma City is a breath of fresh air, compared to the parallel Turner Turnpike. It might take an extra forty-five minutes, but you save the four-dollar toll, and the ride is much more interesting!

Heading west, a classic old steel truss bridge is located between Oklahoma City and Yukon. It's just one of the many classic bridges on Route 66.

This magical route winds past classic structures and through many unique Oklahoma burgs, each having a story of its own. Museums to explore abound. Many of the famous structures such as the Metro Diner on 11th Street in Tulsa are now gone. Fortunately, avant-garde authors, photographers and web masters have captured the priceless images and the soul of the route for new and future generations!

Here's hoping that a Route 66 renaissance will put many small Oklahoma towns back on map and in our hearts, where they belong.

Sue Monkress grew up in the Tulsa, Oklahoma area. She transplanted southward to Gulfport, Mississippi to be closer to her grandchild. She is the author of three books listed on Lulu, is included in the Whortleberry Press 2009 anthology and will be featured in the winter issue of The Oxford So & So.

Discovering Route 66, One Man's Journey

James Piliero

Like many people, my interest in Route 66 goes way back, and has its basis in many years of only cursory knowledge. Sure, growing up I had heard the song and seen the TV show that had first made it recognizable to me as part of our nation's culture. However, these only served to make me aware of its existence. Little did I know that our paths would eventually cross, and one day I'd feel compelled to drive along what is known by such endearing names as "The Mother Road," and "America's Main Street." Route 66's continued status as an American icon is undeniable and even today it has an enduring, even intoxicating, quality that is difficult to deny.

Thanks to the internet, we now have at our disposal the most powerful research tool ever invented, and so this casual interest soon became more detailed. After several months of viewing pictures and reading the stories on-line, it became apparent that a short road trip, at the very least, was inevitable. I set aside a few days, loaded up my Nissan Maxima, and using several books as a guide proceeded to head due north from Dallas until reaching the Missouri/Kansas border.

Soon, I arrived in a different world of small towns, such as Baxter Springs, Kansas, where "Mom and Pop" type establishments, and winding roads which follow the contour of the land, rather than just ramming their way straight through from Point A to Point B, dominated the tree-lined landscape. Here even the Wal-Marts are comparatively small, resembling their ancestry much more than their contemporaries.

What was most remarkable, however, was that everywhere I went, people treated this stranger from "Big D" like family, and went far out of their way to help me in my quest. Nowhere did I notice a lack of recognition or pride in the historical significance of the road along which they lived and worked. This is what Route 66 was, and still is, all about—a continuing legacy of American endurance, pride, and hospitality, which sadly is lost throughout much of the country—now blurred into submission by the pace of our modern society.

Fortunately, we still have one in Route 66, which after all was not at all about speed, but rather more about the sense of adventure traveling by car represents. This is where its true allure lays, both then and now. I realized this by accident while picking my way through all the old alignments.

While I had initially looked forward to seeing the sights and driving along the road of which I'd read so much about beforehand, my attention instead became mesmerized by the excitement of what might potentially lay around each new corner.

You see, Route 66 is rarely straight, includes many right angle turns, and through the years has been realigned in many different configurations, making it perpetually challenging to explore. As my perspective began to change, rather than measuring progress in miles I began instead to measure it by the number of photo opportunities, which are practically limitless.

As the available time began to wane, I realized there was no way anyone could ever hope to see it all, and it was with a deepening sense of despair that I eventually had to turn for home. After four days and over fourteen-hundred miles in the car, I still had not my fill of Route 66, so as a consolation I resolved to visit it again soon. The long drive home on the interstate seemed emptier than usual, further emphasizing the magical quality only the experience of driving along Route 66 can offer.

Upon arriving home, the continued allure of Route 66 was irresistible. As I reviewed the hundreds of photos taken during this first road trip, I soon resolved to return in order to explore even more of its mysterious length.

To date I have already made nearly a dozen trips to the route throughout the past five years, cataloging all I could along the way. These include every state it runs through, with the exception of Arizona. Originally, it had been my intention to drive it all in one marathon journey. However, I soon realized that doing so would cause me to miss much of what I was hoping to see. I've been to its beginning in Chicago, to its end at the Santa Monica Pier, and much of what is in between those two points.

Still, despite all those miles traveled there likely remains much more out there that I may have missed and have yet to see, and I'm looking forward to future trips. Far from being the long, exhausting, typical road trip we in the twenty-first century would prefer to avoid whenever possible, traveling along Route 66 leaves one invigorated by its enduring humanity, appreciation for the landscape, and inescapable sense of humor.

With the benefit of this new perspective, upon reflection I have come to believe that perhaps it is the stark purposefulness and tedium of interstate travel, which makes it seem like such a chore. This continual rush to get from one place to another has eventually served to undermine the great American vacation destination, which was once the road trip. This in turn has continually led us towards the ever larger and more spectacular attraction. By contrast, Route 66's environs are built primarily on a human scale, and designed for a more leisurely pace, which we can still easily appreciate and enjoy.

After all, where else can one go to see a round barn, Cadillacs buried in a field, forests of neon signs, or a blue whale? Of course, these are just the proverbial drop in the bucket, as Route 66 is filled with innumerable sights, sound, and tastes, which can only be found by its side. Strangely, there is something undeniably innocent about all this that reminds us of an America where the pace remains much the same as it did fifty, or even sixty years ago.

Perhaps sleeping in a mock wigwam, attempting to eat a seventy-two ounce steak, or enjoying the countryside view has lost its appeal for many, but not as far as I'm concerned. Before embarking upon my initial trek to Route 66, I thought perhaps I was the only one who still remembered and felt this way. However, after only about five minutes along the route these fears were dispelled, as everywhere, even in nearly abandoned small towns, there were others who felt as I do, and reminders that the people had not forgotten. If they hadn't abandoned that part of the American dream Route 66 once represented, despite being bypassed by new highway construction, how then could I?

I soon learned that the fascination with Route 66 is a worldwide phenomenon. For example, all along the length of my first trip I heard stories about a group of sixty bikers from Norway, who had traveled all the way across the Atlantic Ocean just to experience this American icon for themselves. Of course, this is not surprising, as from its rolling vantage point, you can surely see everything from "amber waves of grain," to "purple mountain's majesty," to the "fruited plains" of lore, making it in many ways the quintessential American experience.

Please bear in mind that I am no expert on this subject by any stretch of the imagination, my sole qualification for writing this is a love for the route, and a sense of mission in campaigning for its continued preservation. This passion for learning all I can about this beloved stretch of road will surely last for the remainder of my life—the essence of Route 66 many people fail to realize.

The fascination with it has never been about the road itself, but rather of the sights and people one encounters along its 2,300 miles. Route 66 belongs to all of us and offers something for nearly everyone. However, unlike other iconic monuments of America's past, such as the Statue of Liberty and the Brooklyn Bridge, neither of which the importance of preservation has ever been seriously questioned, in many places the route has been left to fend for itself against the relentless ravages of time.

The result of this continued apathy will surely be its inevitable decay beyond the point of no return, where what's left merely morphs into the background and is lost forever. Without universal national recognition of Route 66 as a living, enduring symbol of America's past, we stand to lose much more than just a road, but rather an irreplaceable part of our nation's heritage.

James is a graduate of Queens College with a BA in History, and works in marketing for a large manufacturing company based in Ohio. Born and raised in New York, he moved to Texas with his job fifteen years ago. There he first heard about Route 66 and soon began research in earnest. He travels frequently, and since he enjoys writing, this provides him with ample time to do so. His article is an excerpt from a book he recently completed, entitled *The Route*.

Lost On Route 66

66 to 99

Ron Roberson

66 to 99
returning to Pacific time
to the oranges
the packing houses
of the San Joaquin valley
66 to 99
and we're back in Merced County
Jose's five
same age as me
he's Portuguese
Jose threw up
sipping gasoline
from a Pepsi bottle
his father was going to use it
on the carburetor
and there was Karen
Lord
it was all about Karen

Lost On Route 66

we came from the same
Arkansas trees
didn't know I was a cool one
with my blond Californian
calling from the screen
hurry up Oklahoma
slide across the panhandle
no time for Tucumcari
or blue corn and chilies
red and green
in Albuquerque
Daddy can we please?
No we don't stop
for turquoise and jerky
at the border west of Gallup
cut to the future
and I slow for my sun devil waitress
at the Denny's in Holbrook
shrimp salad
a sweet smile
another ice tea
for my table
in the petrified part of Arizona
they say kachinas
live in the San Francisco's
and there's dead chickens for dinner
at the Snow Cap in Seligman
Daddy can we?
No he's tuned to the frequency
of that Ford Fairlane engine
it's going to be a hot climb
when we crawl out of Needles
and there's no refrigerated air
to be found in the Mojave

just the steady breath of hell
coming through the back windows
I recede to the floorboard
and play with the ashtray
flipping it open
flipping it shut
66 to 99
thirty-six hours is about right
to the oranges
the packing houses
where Cesar Chavez
eventually held rallies
66 to 99
and we're back in Merced County
Mom is worried
about the old folks
two-thousand miles behind us
but daddy had his fill of cotton and sawmills
at least out here
he can pay a few bills
and he loved to take us driving
to the high Yosemite
redwoods and waterfalls
we probably saw Ansel Adams
and his god-awful big camera
66 to 99
that's where it all came together

    Ron Robertson's compass usually points southwest when he reaches for another road trip and Route 66 once again is an old friend and a new adventure along the way. His is lucky for having experienced the highway during his youth before the evolution to interstate.

He still explores Route 66 and the surrounding landscape today through photography and film, where he tends to focus on ancient architecture such as Anasazi ruins and roadside desolation. It is great inspiration as well for his songwriting, recording and graphic arts. He lives in the Arkansas Ozarks but home is also all the wonderful trails between there and California.

Lost On Route 66

End of America

Tim Bemis

It is that time of year again when Texas turns from hot to sticky. It's usually when school is over, but I can't figure out when the summer heat arrives anymore. When it does, I know my father is taking his month long camping trip with the rest of the Garland Fire Department.

About a week after the heat struck like a storm, I came home from working at the movie theater to find my father stuffing the back of his Ford pick-up with his camping belongings. Sweat dripped from the underarms of his Navy fire rescue shirt as I watched him from a distance. I walked over to the truck bed and quietly said "Hey Dad," so he couldn't hear me, but he raised his head from the pile of junk and looked at me with dull piercing blue eyes.

"You gonna help me boy?" he said while wiping his forehead.

"If you want me to," I said.

He looked at the pile and then at me like I was an idiot "What do you think? Go inside and get the rest of the shit, retard."

As I walked towards the front door, I saw my brother Jeffy looking out the window at me with a face filled with fear. He gave me a glance then disappeared from the window before I opened the door.

The living room lay cluttered with all of my father's camping essentials; fishing supplies, lamps, tins of food, clothes and probably more. I could care less, except that he didn't need all this for a month of outdoor living. I wanted to burn it all but decided to see what was wrong with my brother instead. When I opened Jeffy's doorway, he had his back to me while he looked out his window.

"You know, you can go outside if you want to."

He turned with tear-filled eyes and stared at me.

"What's wrong?" I said.

"Nothing, I just miss Mom." His answer made me angry because he hadn't known our mother; she died giving birth to him five years ago. I wanted to tell him you can't miss someone you don't know but I just looked at him, thinking of something nice to say until I heard my father yell.

"Junior, where the fuck are you? I thought you were gonna help me!"

I hated when he called me junior. Just because we share the same name doesn't mean he can call me that. I walked outside and threw him his tackle box.

"Don't call me Junior, Dad."
"What? That's your name."
"No, it's Marcus."
"Yeah, Marcus Jr."
"Just Marcus, Dad." I went inside and back to Jeffy's room before he could toss another wisecrack my way.
"So what's wrong, Jeffy?"
"I can't say."
"Why not? We're brothers. We should tell each other everything."
He turned away from me and looked out the window again.
"Dad got mad at me."
"Oh, that's no big deal," I said. I put my hands on his shoulders and leaned forward so our faces were side by side. "He's always getting mad at me."
"Ow!" Jeffy flinched at my touch and I stood up straight and backed away slowly from him.
"What's wrong?"
"You hurt my shoulder."
"Sorry. I didn't think I was pushing that hard, let me see." Jeffy immediately climbed on his bed and got under the covers.
"Why are you acting so weird?"
When I lifted the covers, I could see he was in a ball of protection. I told him I only wanted to see where it hurt but he still wouldn't show me, so I pulled his shirt collar down to his shoulder and saw a dark purple bruise.
"Dad do this to you?"
"No! I fell today, that's why he got mad."
"Come out from under the covers." He didn't follow me right away but after a few minutes, he

did because he knew I wasn't going anywhere. As soon as he was on two feet, I took off his shirt and found four more bruises on his torso. He held his pudgy stomach like a safety raft as I walked around him.

"Can I put my shirt back on now?"

When he said this, I felt his discomfort and let him. "Tell the truth. Did Dad do this?"

"No! Me and my friends have been wrestling lately that's all."

"Then why were you crying? And why did you say that you made Dad mad?" I had caught him in his lie, as I watched him sweat, searching for an answer, I felt like a parent more than a brother, but this was something I had to do.

I wasn't ready for Jeffy to break down. I thought he would just give me a simple answer, but instead I got a sobbing mess.

"Yes . . . he . . . he . . . did . . . it," Jeffy blubbered. I got down on one knee so we were at eye level.

"How long?"

"I . . . don't . . . know."

Jeffy couldn't look at me anymore. He was crying, his eyes fixated on the floor as his sobbing grew louder.

"It's ok," I said, hugging him. "He's not going to hurt you anymore."

When I told him to relax and put him in bed, I could tell he felt a little safer. I closed his door gently and walked over to the pile of camping supplies, grabbed as much junk as I could carry and took it to the truck.

"That's it boy! Now you are working!"

I didn't even look at the sonofabitch; the only thing that was on my mind was load, load, and load. When the truck was ready to go my father started toward the front door but I stopped him.

"Don't you need to get going?"

"I wanna say goodbye to Jeffy first."

Don't you mean give him a few goodbye swings? I wanted to say. Instead, I told him that Jeffy was sleeping so he turned around and got into his truck. Before he drove away, he yelled out the window.

"You boys behave! Take good care of Jeffy, Junior!"

"My name is not Junior."

My father ignored my last statement and drove off toward the Texas sun.

The next hour felt like only minutes, as I packed all of my favorite clothes, ransacked my father's room and came out with a thousand dollars I found underneath his mattress. Jeffy and I were moving to California to get away from the bastard. I called my best friend, Yoyo, to ask him if he wanted to come for the ride, then woke up Jeffy, telling him to help me pack his clothes because we were moving. He watched me throw a bunch of his clothes in a suitcase for a few moments, then started asking questions.

"Why are we moving?"

"Because Dad is mean to you and me."

"We're running away from Dad?"

"Yeah, that's what we're doing, now get up."

Jeffy wasn't upset anymore, but he kept asking questions while we packed his clothes. I shut him up after about three minutes by telling him Yoyo was coming with us.

"Yoyo? Oh man! Yoyo's the coolest," he said with joy.

Me and Jeffy put our suitcases in the trunk of my ten year-old car, a white fifty-six Renault Dauphine. Took one last look at the house we spent our entire lives in, and then drove across town to Yoyo's house. Yoyo was sitting on his porch when we pulled up; his shoulder-length hair blew in the breeze while his white aviators reflected the sunlight.

"Yoyo!" Jeffy yelled out the window as I put the car in park, I knew Yoyo was irritated because I didn't tell him Jeffy was coming with us. He sat in his lawn chair staring into the distance. At least it looked that way as we walked up to him.

"Why'd you bring the runt?" He dug into his cutoff shorts, pulled out a bowl with a bag and began to pack it with marijuana. I took the bowl away before he could finish.

"What gives, Marcus?"

"Not in front of my brother."

"So you expect me to sneak around the whole trip so porky doesn't see me?" We had a stare off until Jeffy asked what that thing was that Yoyo pulled out of his pocket. "Nothing" Yoyo said quickly. "You ready to go to California?"

"California? Is that where we're going?" Jeffy said in a high voice.

"Yeah, taking ol' 66 to Cali," Yoyo replied in a cool fashion while Jeffy looked confused.

"You got all your shit packed?" I asked.

"Yep it's inside, just waiting on you, boss."

"Your parents aren't upset you're just up and leaving for California?"

Yoyo tipped his glasses down and looked at me, scrutinizing, as if I were a space alien. I should have known that during the number of years Yoyo and I were friends his parents never gave two shits about him.

"Can I use your phone?"

"Yeah it's in the kitchen."

I needed to call my girlfriend, Lily, to ask her a very important question. If she didn't say yes then our two and a half year relationship was just for shits and giggles.

"Lily? Hey, it's Marcus." I paused a moment, wiping sweaty palms on my jeans. "Will you go to California with me, Yoyo and Jeffy?"

She laughed awkwardly; calling me crazy, she told me her parents would kill her if she took off for California.

"C'mon Lily, there's nothing they can do, you're nineteen. Just come, it'll be fun," I said.

She asked when we were coming back to Garland, like we were going on vacation, and I started getting annoyed.

"I don't know, you're thinking too far ahead! Just pack a bunch of clothes and get a hold of as much money as you can and meet me down the street at Yoyo's in a few minutes, okay?"

Her voice sounded strained as if she was on the verge of crying after she said okay so I told her I loved her and hung up the phone.

When I walked out to the porch Yoyo was sitting, watching Jeffy poke a beehive in the neighbor's yard with a stick. I ran over frantically and picked him up before he took a swing and ran back to Yoyo's yard.

"Why didn't you stop him?" I screamed at Yoyo.

"He looked like he was having fun," he replied with a smirk.

Jeffy squirmed under my arm and said, "Yoyo told me it was a piñata filled with candy."

I dropped Jeffy like a duffle bag, rushed up to the porch and got in Yoyo's face.

"You could have killed him, you asshole! If you are going to be like this the whole time you can fucking stay! I got one five year old to take care of! I don't need two!"

I stayed in his face like a mean-spirited drill sergeant waiting for a reply, but Lily's voice interrupted my stare.

"Just kiss, I know you two are dying to do it."

She stood on the lawn still holding her suitcase, she wore short shorts and a white button-up shirt tied in a knot so you could see her stomach glistening from the heat. She had her hair in a bob that looked new to me but it made her look ten times as sexy. A blonde with a bob just screamed sexy to me.

Jeffy gave Lily a hug and asked if she was coming to California with us. She nodded while messing up his hair, something she always did when she saw him.

"Let's go!" Jeffy said as if he was leader of the pack and climbed into the front seat of the Dauphine.

Lily and I laughed as we held each other, then Lily got serious and asked why I wanted to go to

California. I looked at Jeffy leaning out the window, waiting for the adventure to begin and said that I would tell her later.

"C'mon dipstick. Get outta the front, you are riding in back with me."

Yoyo appeared with his bag hanging on his right shoulder and an acoustic guitar strapped around him, looking like a traveling mariachi. He walked up to us, still wearing his aviators.

"Bowl me." I gave him his bowl and he put it in his pocket and started talking again. "So what's the plan here?"

I looked at Lily and Jeffy to make sure they were paying attention, took out a map, put it on the hood of the Dauphine and began showing them the route we were taking.

"First we go to Amarillo. From there we jump on Route 66 and head west, going through New Mexico, Arizona and then California."

"So we just go west on 66 the whole time?" Lily asked.

"Yep, until we get to California. Should take us about twenty-four hours. Maybe a little longer. So is everybody ready?"

Lily and Yoyo nodded their heads while Jeffy screamed "Yeah!"

I put Lily and Yoyo's bags in the trunk and we began our journey toward the Mother Road, Route 66, leaving Garland and the hot weather of Texas behind.

The Dauphine wasn't the best car to travel in but it was all we had. It was, in fact, a real piece of shit. It took about thirty seconds to get up to sixty on the highway. Everyone thought something was wrong with the motor, but I knew otherwise. Jeffy watched everything fly by the window, like a dog that got to go for a ride, while the rest of us talked as I navigated the rust bucket towards Route 66. Lily turned in her seat and asked Yoyo why he wanted to go to California.

"I'm gonna try and make it as a musician, like Dylan," he said simply while strumming his guitar.

"Yoyo the hippie!" Lily roared. Making us all laugh.

"Real funny. I ain't gonna be known as Yoyo. And I aint no fuckin' hippie either! Stupid hippies, protesting Vietnam. Been going on for years and I'm sick of it!"

"All right, then, Yoyo the mariachi," Lily said to end Yoyo's rant. "How did you get stuck with that goofy name anyways?"

"In third grade when our teacher was taking attendance he would say Alex Yoapo and when he said Yoapo fast it sounds like Yoyo."

"Yep, and from then on he was known to everyone as Yoyo," I said with a chuckle.

"Why do you wanna go to California?" Yoyo asked Lily.

"I don't really know, I was kinda rushed into making the decision, but I guess I've always wanted to go there."

She turned and faced the road then started rubbing my arm. The only sound was the plucking of Yoyo's guitar stings after that, until we got on Route 66. Jeffy yelled with excitement and we all smiled at his reaction.

We stopped at a diner called Sandy's somewhere in New Mexico right off 66 that was next to a place that sold fireworks. When we all got out of the car, I could see every man in the parking lot looking at Lily, their eyes fixated on her lithe body packed into short shorts. Lily didn't notice at first but finally asked why they were staring.

"Cause they all wanna fuck you," Yoyo blurted out.

"What?" she said in shock as she glanced around the diner.

I slouched in the booth, grumbling to myself in a jealous rage. Yoyo noticed and tried to make me feel better.

"You should take it as a compliment, everyone wants your girl but it's you who's going home with her at the end of the night."

"Yeah, I guess," I said.

It still bothered me that all these pigs were eye-fucking my girlfriend, fantasizing about taking her to a dirty stall in the bathroom before their food came. As these thoughts were going through my mind, a waitress brought over some coffee and a man in a white mobster hat spoke to Lily from the booth behind us.

"Sorry to interrupt you miss, but I wanted to tell you that you are very beautiful."

He said this in a Spanish accent.

"Oh, well thank you."

Lily's face started turning red and so did mine as I turned to get a look at the person I perceived as a scumbag. He had a dark brown complexion along with a dirty black mustache. He glanced at me and paid no attention that I was staring and continued talking to Lily.

"So have you ever thought about being in pictures?"

"You gotta be kidding," she said while giggling like a schoolgirl.

"Well, you'd be perfect."

"We're heading to California so I'll be right in the neighborhood!"

"Is that so?" he said with wide eyes. "Take my card and give me a call. We'll work something out."

Lily turned back to our booth holding the card. She was star struck and I was still trying to fathom what just happened, until I noticed Jeffy drinking coffee like water.

"Jeffy, no more!"

He stopped and licked his lips. "You are right Yoyo. That is good!"

Yoyo laughed and sipped his coffee. The rest of our meal I kept quiet and watched Lily looking at the card, frightened for the future. When we got up to leave, the Spanish man that looked like a mobster told Lily to call him.

"I will, Antonio."

"Please, call me Tony."

"It has a name?" I said to Lily with a snort.

I followed her when she stormed out of the diner.

"He's a movie producer and can make me a star. Why do you want to ruin it for me?"

"I'm not ruining anything. The guy's obviously telling you what you want to hear."

Yoyo was behind the rust bucket motioning that him and Jeffy were going to the fireworks store; I nodded and continued to argue with Lily.

"He's only saying that to get in your pants!"

"I can't believe you, Marcus. He only wants to help me!"

"Since when did you want to be a star?"

I saw in the corner of my eye Yoyo brushing past a hippie holding a sign that said "fireworks kill."

"Who doesn't want to be a star? I didn't have any reason to go to California and now I do!" she said.

"I thought your reason was to be with me!"

"I don't even know why you're going!"

"Because Dad beats Jeffy, that's why! I had to get him out of that house!"

Lily grew silent and began to walk towards the back of the rust bucket.

"It's a big world outside of Garland, and I'm done missing out on it."

She tried to open the trunk to get her suitcase but found it locked.

"We're out of Garland. We can start a new life, together," I said.

"Same life, just a different state. I want more, not baby-sit you Jeffy and Yoyo. Now give me the keys."

"And all of this popped into your head after that con artist inside told you about the wonders of Hollywood?"

"He's not a con artist, but yes, he opened my eyes to a world I never thought I could be involved in, and now I have a chance."

I unlocked the trunk.

"You are gonna regret this," I said.

"Yeah, right. Best decision I've made in two years."

Lily lugged her suitcase into the diner and I walked over to the fireworks store, choking back as many tears as I could. I almost told her I loved her in the hope it would make her stay, but realized it would make no difference.

Yoyo, Jeffy, grinning ear to ear, right behind him, was walking out of the store. I was still a distance away but I could see and hear them perfectly.

The hippie outside of the store walked up to Yoyo and said, "Mother Earth can't take all that polluted smoke man. Stop polluting it."

Yoyo dropped the bag of fireworks and punched him in the face. Inexplicably, it cheered me up after the blowout I'd had with Lily. Yoyo was staring at the hippie, ready to hit him again when I walked up.

"How's Lily?" he asked.

We both looked over at the diner parking lot as she stuffed her suitcase in the back seat of the man's white Cadillac convertible.

"Gone," I said, tears welling in my eyes.

We were close to Arizona when Jeffy saw a buzzing neon sign saying Teepee Lodge. That night, we checked into a hotel shaped like a teepee. I didn't really mind stopping. Droned out from the day, I needed the rest.

The night didn't involve much sleeping and consisted of me and Yoyo waiting for Jeffy to fall asleep. When he finally did, we proceeded to get stone drunk off a bottle of tequila Yoyo had in his bag. Around one in the morning, we saw a small Indian woman with long black hair and wearing a denim vest and bell-bottoms getting ice outside our door.

"You looking for a good time?" Yoyo slurred as we approached the woman. She didn't reply, so he kept talking. "Here's a real good piece of ass lady, he'll fuck you real good!"

I assumed that Yoyo was referring to me; being just as drunk, I decided to play along.

"Ya! I'll show you a great time baby! Fuck you right in the bathroom over there!"

The Indian woman looked frightened. She gripped her ice bucket and continued to stare.

"C'mon man, let's get out of here! This Indian slut won't put out."

We started walking away but as we did, I looked behind me at the woman, staring at us with an expression of pure terror. Drunk as I was, I couldn't help but feel ashamed.

Shaking my head, I said, "It was only a matter of time."

The rest of the night we lit bottle rockets on the roof, and put cherry bombs in all the public toilets of the lodge a half hour before sunrise. It was all in good fun but it didn't mend my heart from Lily's departure, or the growing disgust I felt in myself.

* * *

Arizona is a beautiful state and I soon forgot the prior night and began to feel as if my life was taking a new direction. I wondered if Jeffy and Yoyo felt the same as desert air rolled off the rust bucket and into our souls as we motored past places like the Grand Canyon, Painted Desert and the Wild West mining town of Oatman.

None of us was very interested so we didn't stop. He was more concentrated on firing roman candles at cars when me and Yoyo weren't paying attention. We'd had our fun last night, so why couldn't he?

We did stop at the world's largest sundial. It was sixty-two feet wide and pointed straight to the North Star. At least that's what the sign said. As all three of us stood on the sundial, I thought about how precious time is. I never realized how fast everything in my life had passed me by until that moment at the sundial. For the first time, I felt less than invincible.

We stopped at one more tourist trap on the outskirts of California; Yoyo grabbed the wheel once he saw a bright green building that said "Freak Show" on it. While turning the rust bucket into the parking lot, I debated whether the creatures inside were real or just hoaxes. A man in a beat up bowler cap and a dusty black suit stepped outside the doors once we got out of the car.

"Howdy chums," he said in a high-droning voice. "Come to see the freak?" Yoyo gave the man a "hell yeah!" for an answer while Jeffy and I looked at him and the building strangely, not knowing what to do or believe.

"Well you came to the right place chums! Follow me!"

The excited man danced as he led us into the building, acting more like a cartoon character than human. It made Jeffy laugh. We each paid a dollar and he led us to the second floor of the building, Yoyo as anxious as a kid at Christmas.

"Behind this door is pure evil; I picked up the freak a few years ago in Kentucky and he is devil cursed. Be quiet when going in 'cause you don't want to wake him." The man opened the door slowly. Knock when you're ready to come out."

The large room had tall stacks of unknown debris covered in white sheets. I peeked beneath one. Boxes, nothing strange, I thought, but who knows what was under every sheet. We walked slowly and with caution toward the middle of the room. Jeffy kept close to me while Yoyo and I looked around for something out of the ordinary.

Sun shining into the room made all the dust in the air visible. It seemed like no one had been there for years. I thought white sheets covered all of the piles until I saw a large box-like shape covered with a black sheet. It was about ten feet away from us and I knew that was what the man wanted us to see. The box was almost as tall as Jeffy, and about six feet long.

"Take it off" Yoyo said to me.

"Not me. You're the one who wanted to see it."

Yoyo grabbed the black cover while Jeffy and I stepped back a few feet. What was under it was a man, but not like any man I ever saw. His torso and stomach looked twisted like taffy, accompanied with boils all over and a face that looked like there was a softball lodged inside it. Jeffy covered his eyes in horror while Yoyo looked shocked and entertained all rolled into one.

"What's wrong with him?" Jeffy asked. Me and Yoyo looked at each other and said, "Agent Orange."

Jeffy asked what Agent Orange was but we told him we'd tell him about it when he was older. We didn't stare at the man too long. For me the longer I looked the worse I felt. Yoyo covered the cage and we walked back to the door and knocked on it. The man in the bowler hat appeared and a crazy grin formed on his face when he saw ours.

"You boys look shook up. Get your money's worth?"

We didn't answer him as we returned to the rust bucket in robotic motion. I started the car and we drove off towards California. About a half hour later Jeffy started crying abruptly, it finally sunk in for him. Our road trip was almost over.

Good ol' 66 was near its end and everything we went through was worth it once the rust bucket was on Santa Monica Boulevard. It led through Hollywood, Beverly Hills and finally to the Santa Monica Pier on the Pacific Ocean.

I parked close to the pier and we got out and walked. Jeffy noticed a carnival at the end of the pier facing the ocean. We rode the Ferris wheel so we could watch the sun sink into the pacific, sitting quietly when our car halted at the top. I never imagined beauty like this existed. Everything felt so surreal, like a dream that I didn't want to end.

Reality closed in when Jeffy asked, "So what are we gonna do now that we're here?"

"Enjoy the view until I think of something," I said.

Yoyo glanced away from the sunset and said, "You don't know do you?"

I didn't have an answer, and just kept staring at the horizon ablaze in color, wishing reality would never return to haunt me.

Tim Bemis has a Bachelors degree in Creative Writing, and is currently working on getting his Master's in Fiction Writing. In his spare time, besides writing, he enjoys making music, reading, and watching films. He lives in Hooksett, New Hampshire.

Are There Many Trains in Gallup?

Margaret Melloy Guziak

 We left San Diego bound for Colorado when a torrential rainstorm in New Mexico forced us to stop on Route 66 at a Gallup motel. Our sleeping bags and extra suitcases were soaked in the luggage rack atop our nine-passenger Buick station wagon. The three kids were sprawled across the seats, sleeping upright in "pre-seatbelt days." My husband pulled up next to the red neon, flashing vacancy sign on the office window.
 Holding a newspaper over my head, I hurried into the darkened, smoky office where a straggly-haired woman who resembled one of Shakespeare's three witches confronted me. Laying her cigarette down in the ashtray after inhaling one last, deep puff, she slid a metal key and the grimy desk blotter across the counter for me to sign in.

When I asked if I could see the room first, her skeletal right hand snatched back the key and the blotter as she snarled four words at me.

"Want it or don'cha?"

"I want it. It's pouring outside," I replied anxiously, signing the register.

Outside, a train whistle blew, threatening to shatter the window as its wheels "clickety-clacked" across the street on its way through town.

"Are there many trains in Gallup?" I asked her, innocently, as I opened the crusty outer door.

"Some. Don't have to worry none though," she cackled, "only if you hear a real long whistle. Means an Indian from the Rez is walking home. If he falls down on the track, the engineer blows the whistle just one time. And if he doesn't get up in time, well," she ended in mid-sentence, slapping her rough, bony hands one against the other.

Returning to the car clutching the room key, I climbed in and announced, "Room 10."

Ray backed up to the parking space outside the room. We gently woke the kids and shepherded them inside to take off their shoes and climb into bed, promising them a delicious breakfast in the morning.

The shabby, dark green, uneven curtains couldn't muffle out the rain's sound or the occasional flash of desert lightning. Heavy rain continued to pelt our motel room's front window, while trains rolled through Gallup. The whistles blew loud and long.

"Oh, please. Oh, please get up off the track," I prayed silently, remembering what she had confessed to me.

The next morning, with a bright New Mexico sky overhead, we pulled out, splashing our car across the deep, rain-filled potholes of the parking lot. At breakfast at a diner down Route 66, I told my husband what the old woman had said and how tired I was because I was awake most of the night, praying for the Indians to get off the track whenever I heard the train whistle blow.

"And you actually believed her?" Over his plate of ham and eggs, he scoffed at my naiveté, shaking his head. "Probably pulls that on lots of people. Bet it was her laugh for the day. She must have seen our California plates."

Margaret has lived in five western states and traveled extensively with her husband throughout the Midwest and the west. She is the author of *Burnin' Daylight—a Fun Wild West Quiz*. The book is available at www.booklocker.com. A freelance writer, she grew up in the east but currently resides on nearly four acres of land in western Colorado.

I Got My Grapefruit on Route 66

Elizabeth Rogge

It really was a dark and stormy night when the blizzard blew into town, swirling snow in every direction like a crazy white tornado and blanketing Route 66 with a whiteout. Winter had come to Gallup.

***

After graduating from nursing school, I took a train from Hartford, Connecticut to Gallup, New Mexico to start my first job as a nurse at the Public Health Service Indian Hospital (now known as Gallup Indian Medical Center). I had been in town about two month before the intense winter storm slowed and then finally halted the traffic along Route 66.

***

The next morning, while at work at the hospital, one of my colleagues received a phone call from her husband.

"What? Are you serious?" Joan asked. "Okay, I'll tell them and we'll be down after work." Joan hung up the phone and turned toward me. "Do you like grapefruit?"

"Yes," I replied, "why?"

"Well, there's a whole truckload waiting for us to pick up after work."

I was bewildered. "What? Where did it come from?"

"A semi loaded with grapefruit jack-knifed, west of town, and is sitting off the side of the road. Since the driver can't go anywhere until after the storm lets up, his company told him to give the grapefruit away before it freezes. Jim (Joan's husband was a highway patrolman) thought it would be a nice surprise for us nurses."

After some of the grapefruit was given to the nursing home, there was plenty left over to distribute to the nursing staff at the hospital. I was sweetly rewarded that day with a bushel of grapefruit.

***

Back in 1961, many people got their "kicks on Route 66," but I got my grapefruit there.

Elizabeth Rogge is a retired registered nurse whose published works include short stories, poetry, and a weekly newspaper column. She traveled throughout the United States and around the world before settling in Kansas where she now lives with her husband and continues to write WritingsByElizabeth.wordpress.com is her blog.

Old Route 66

Jo Gray

Arizona has the longest stretch of Route 66 still in use. The city of Kingman is the mid-point of the legendary road. It is here the old Route 66 is named Andy Devine Avenue, after the well-known Hollywood actor.

Andy was born in Flagstaff, Arizona, on October 7, 1905, to Thomas and Amy Devine. Thomas worked as a locomotive fireman and blacksmith for the lumber company railroad in Flagstaff. A railroad accident cost him a leg and his job.

Thomas met and courted Amy Ward while recuperating in the hospital. The pair married, started a family and settled into Flagstaff life.

Using accident settlement money and earnings from serving as county recorder, Thomas moved his family to Kingman, a railroad town in the northwest corner of Arizona. There, he purchased the two-story Hotel Beale on Front Street opposite the Kingman train station and the Santa Fe Railroad's Harvey House restaurant. It was here young Andy, his half-sister May, and older brother, Tom, Jr., grew up.

Andy and Tom usually worked at the Hotel Beale, but during summers, Andy would cowboy on local ranches. It was at one of the Kingman ranches in the summer of 1919 that Andy was first exposed to the movie business.

The famous director, John Ford, was filming a western, "Ace of the Saddle," starring Harry Carey. The film was being shot on the ranch where Andy worked. Andy got a day's work as an extra.

Seven years later, Andy was standing on a street corner in Hollywood wearing a varsity athlete jacket from a northern Arizona college. He was approached by an assistant director at Universal Pictures. The jacket worn by Andy indicated the young man was familiar with the game of football. The director was looking for football players to be in a series of films being shot at Universal.

The series was called "The Collegians," and the football player was told he might get several weeks of work from the film series. Several weeks turned into a lifetime for Andy Devine, who was best known as the comic sidekick in countless westerns, where his voice—half squeak, half rasp—became his trademark.

The voice, which might have cost another actor a career, ironically led to Andy's success and popularity. Once heard, his voice was never forgotten.

According to Andy's late wife, Dorothy (Doagie), the voice was the result of an accident when Andy was a child of six or seven. He was pretending to be a "hero" while jumping up and down on the sofa with a stick from the bottom of a window shade in his mouth. Young Andy fell with the stick lodged there.

"Dad said he was never quite sure if that incident was what gave his voice its unique sound, but it was an explanation. He wasn't going to complain about something that became a meal ticket," Tad Devine recalled.

Andy played Jingle Jones, the comic relief sidekick to Guy Madison's Marshal James Butler in "The Adventures of Wild Bill Hickok" from 1951 to 1958.

The TV series was still running when Andy took over as host of a children's television series, "Andy's Gang." Who from that era can forget, "Pluck your magic twanger, Froggie," Andy's oft-used line?

Though battling a chronic form of leukemia for years, Andy remained active and retained his good-natured personality to the day he died of cardiac arrest—February 18, 1977.

Kingman, Arizona celebrates the hometown star each September with Andy Devine Days. The celebration consists of a parade and a rodeo.

An article written by Karen Goudy for the city's museum of history and arts website, www.fitlink.net/mocohis/museum/andy, explains the town's pride.

"We in Kingman, celebrate Andy Devine Days, partly because he was a famous movie star, but primarily because he was one of our own, a decent, caring man who took what gifts he had and built a life to be proud of."

Jo Gray is a freelance writer, living in Kingman, Arizona on old Route 66.

Lost On Route 66
A day in the life of a forensic death investigator

G. Terry Felts

Mornings greets each of us differently, if only by degrees. The coolness of the exposed sheet as your foot stretches out from underneath the cover toward the edge of the bed invigorates your soul while stimulating your eyelids to open wide as your lungs suck in your first cognizant breath of the day. The reality is that it is just your next breath and while a good sleep refreshes and renews your body and spirit, the sins of your past rapidly flood back into perspective, triggering your feet to hit the floor as you drag your ass to the shower to begin another day.

Before I'm dressed, a call from the local sheriff comes in advising an elderly resident woke up dead. The death appears natural but the deceased hasn't seen a doctor in years so the death is therefore unattended and becomes a Medical Examiner case. Especially grieving loved ones, dutifully at the deceased's side when they crossed over, sometimes misconstrue the term unattended. Offended by the inference they were absent at the end, you have to carefully explain the term "unattended" refers to the deceased being unattended by a doctor.

Grabbing camera and notebook and kissing my wife good-bye, I begin the twenty-five mile drive down Route 66 to the deceased's residence.

It's not the first such drive I've made on the Mother Road, or the last. Old 66 always gave me a serenity that the Interstate didn't as I made my way to the end of the trail for so many over the years.

On arrival, a deputy advises me that the deceased's daughter discovered her body after several unsuccessful attempts to contact her by phone. The daughter reported her mother had complained of heartburn the prior evening and had gone to bed early. The residence was secure when the daughter arrived and she turned the alarm off after entering the home.

The deceased's car is in the garage and the home is clean and orderly. A barely touched dinner of baked chicken, scalloped potatoes and green beans is on the kitchen counter next to the sink. Only empty packages of Rolaids, a glass of water and TV remote control are on the table next to the deceased's chair in the living room.

Upon entering the bedroom, we find the deceased on the bed, covers and sleepwear appropriately in place. There is a bottle of Pepto Bismol and a washcloth on the bedside table next to the telephone. The deceased is lying on her right side. An examination of the bathroom reveals no prescription medication, only over-the-counter meds such as aspirin, antibiotic ointment and miscellaneous hygiene products. The toilet bowl contains vomit from the partially eaten dinner.

The deputy and I return to the body where I remove the sleepwear and position the remains to perform an external exam. As a death investigator, I rely on several observations during this procedure. In a trauma free exam, we rely on the mortis sisters—rigor, livor and algor—to provide clues.

In the case at hand, livor was consistent with the position in which I found the body, and rigor consistent with death occurring between the last reported time seen alive and time discovered. Algor indicated the death had occurred approximately ten hours earlier. I then drew vitreous humor from eyes, femoral blood and urine. The deputy and I sat with the deceased's daughter while waiting for the local funeral home to remove the body.

I usually found that my words of comfort, no matter how trite, were better than none at all.

Pulling back out on the Mother Road, I headed home, listening to the breaks in the concrete click under the car, I wondered if the deceased had any idea of her failing physical condition prior to her death at sixty years of age. I speculated if regular doctor visits would have extended her life or if it was just her time. We humans tend to become complacent with our health, too often thinking, "When it's your time, it's your time."

My own doctor advised me as much thirty years earlier when he first prescribed medication for my elevated blood pressure.

"Lose thirty pounds and you won't need these anymore."

My response was to gain thirty more pounds over the following years. More than one stop at the fried food counters of the gas and rest stops along the Mother Road had seen to that.

As I pulled off the highway back into my own driveway, I summed up my internal inquiry by telling myself fifteen, or even ten more years wouldn't be so bad and remembering I had told my wife a few days earlier I wanted the Grateful Dead lyrics, *What a Long Strange Trip it Has Been,* etched into my urn.

Maybe I need to walk a little more often and drink a little less. Of one thing I'm sure, it seems fair to me that death investigators should be able to write off the cost of their favorite alcoholic beverage.

G. Terry Felts is a licensed private investigator. He has worked as an operating room assistant, a police officer, petroleum landman and owner of Alpha Energy Corp. He was also Field Death Investigator for four counties in Oklahoma and investigated more than one thousand deaths. He worked on the scene with the Medical Examiner's office during the Murrah Building bombing of 1995, and again during the chaotic aftermath of the

F5 tornado of 1999 that destroyed the City of Moore.

He holds an AS in Police Science (OSU), a BA in Criminal Justice (UCO) and an MA in Criminal Justice Management and Administration (UCO). He and his wife Deborah own and operate ISystems, LLC that finds lost mineral owners and their heirs, and Private Autopsy Service, LLC.

Hitchhiker

Jack Horne

I wondered why I'd flagged her down -
She looked a mess and acted weird;
She talked about the deaths she'd watched
And roared with laughter as she steered.

I said I didn't want to know
About the accidents she'd seen;
She told me, 'Hell, I'm having fun.'
And, 'Get out then if I'm so mean!'

At last I said, 'I get out here.'
—I hoped to thumb another ride—
She let me out and laughed again,
And told me, 'This is where I died.'

She vanished then before my eyes.
As thunder rolled and lightning flashed,
I slowly walked towards *my spot*:
The place I'd died, where I had crashed.

Jack is married and works for the theatre in Plymouth, England. He has had stories, poems, and articles published in magazines in the UK and USA

Pauline's Bait and Tackle

Janet Galloway

(Photo of Pauline's Bait and Tackle, circa 1981. Used with permission of The Oklahoman)

Lost On Route 66

I have a whole treasure chest of memories from Pauline's Bait House, a wonderful place that sat just south of historic Route 66. I must have been in that glorious stage of my early twenties. Every weekend I rode my Arabian stallion on a fifteen-mile trek around Lake Overholser. By the time I got to Pauline's that ice-cold longneck Bud sure hit the spot. The onion-fried hamburgers were the best in the world.

When I first started going there, it was a relatively quiet place. The hum of the ancient ceiling fans could even be heard with blades so dusty it resembled Spanish moss floating in slow circles beneath. Usually there were just some older guys sitting around playing dominoes and telling fish stories. They might have been bragging about how the alligator gar on the wall had been caught by their granddad. Or maybe the buck with the biggest rack came from the creek in back of their house. There was about every Oklahoma native creature you could imagine, and then some, stuffed, mounted and displayed in that place. From the full-sized alligator to the coons and the badgers, the baby bear holding a beer bottle, sometimes you had to wonder if they came alive and partied when the doors closed at night. My favorite was the five-piece bullfrog band that sat on a shelf behind the bar. Frozen in time, perhaps in another dimension, they each held a frog-sized musical instrument.

By the time *Urban Cowboy* hit the silver screen, and the two-step became as popular as the twist, word started getting around about the quaint and unusual bait house. It got to where on Sundays it was standing room only, and Pauline's little hand-scribbled warnings about crushing beer cans and sitting on the tables were hard for her to enforce.

I had never before or since heard such soulful yodeling as when Wesley was up on the little bandstand singing "Cattle Call." When Booker T sang "Kalijah," I swear the minnows would leap right out of the water like tiny dolphins. There was a hitching post just outside the front door where we usually parked our horses. When the parking lot became jammed with everything from redneck four-wheel drives to Harley Hogs, we opted to tie the horses to the fence near the back.

I always admired Teresa, she was so cute and Bruce worshipped the ground she walked on. Of course, we were all in love back then. We were young and full of life and living it to the fullest. Teresa had a big old gelding that must have been part thoroughbred. His name was Honky-tonk. I know Bruce was never the same after she got killed. Could have happened to me just as easy, but by the grace of God here I sit, with all these old memories swimming around in my head.

When my California sister came back to Oklahoma for a visit, her Englishman husband accompanied her. I put them both on horses and off to Pauline's we rode. They'd never had an experience like that! What a ball we had: Oklahoma cowboys and cowgirls, Pauline style. That day is permanently etched in our minds, not to be forgotten until we're laid to rest. The bait house was like no other; anywhere, anytime; any space or planet. Pauline's was a one in a million, never again to be reproduced. If you weren't there in that particular era, you missed it. Like a shooting star, you were lucky enough to see, only because you happened to step outside on a starlit night.

Half the time the sunset snuck up on us, and we'd have to ride home in the dark. The horses knew the way and it's probably a good thing, 'cause sometimes our navigation system was a bit cloudy after a day of riding, dancing and drinking. We would have sparks shooting off the shoes of our horses crossing that old Highway 66 Bridge. It had a steel joint in it that clanked so loud that when a car ran over it, you could hear it half a mile away. You had to time your horse's pace to avoid it when the inconsiderate lake traffic insisted on crowding in on that skinny bridge with us. It is a wonder I am still here to share these memories with you. I hope the ones who were there will get a kick out my recollection—somewhat like putting color on an old black and white movie.

There was Poopsie and Mary Anne, Gene and Patsy, and of course Pauline and Teresa. There were younger regulars also—Bruce and Richard and Larry, and Bob, Ronny and Jerry and Stanley and that crew. There were many others, myself included—the laughing redhead on her faithful steed, with her handsome husband always by her side—the two who were misplaced in time.

Daddy always said I should have been born a century earlier. For the ones that missed it, I'm sincerely sorry. Pauline's was nothing short of a historical monument, and the souls within were all folk heroes. Though many of them have departed this earth, they will always be alive in my heart.

Janet Galloway is a native Oklahoman, and the youngest of five children. Her close-knit family has roots in Oklahoma City and all her siblings pursued their education in Oklahoma as well. She married her high school sweetheart but was widowed on her twenty-ninth birthday and never remarried. Janet has enjoyed trying her hand at many things and has always found a challenge around every corner. She has worked many trades including real estate appraising, welding, plumbing, remodeling, and even heat and air. She has been a gourmet chef and an Emergency Medical Technician.

She is an accomplished artist and does commissioned portraits of dogs and horses. Throughout her assorted careers, Janet has bred, raised and trained Arabian horses for over thirty years. She is a Preservation Breeder of a specific early American Champion bloodline. She is on the Board of Directors of the Oklahoma Arabian Horse Club and writes a regular column for the club newsletter. She now lives outside of Norman Oklahoma with her loyal Old English Mastiff named Doc and her prized Arabian horses.

Pop Hick's, America's Kitchen

Luke Black

It was 1998 and I was an arrogant college freshman living three-hundred miles from home in the wind-swept plains of Weatherford, Oklahoma. Like many green students drunk on freedom, I had slipped into a lackadaisical coma of procrastination. While it is common for college freshmen to experiment with varied levels of academic delinquency before finding a healthy balance of responsibility and freedom, I never did. Instead, I embraced a philosophy of complete irresponsibility, finely honed to a razor's edge.

The true absurdity of my reasoning was not fully realized until the semester's end, one night before my first final. The moon hung high when the reality of consequence flashed in my brain like a bright, white bulb. I had some serious studying to do and only one miserable night to do it.

After a while of aimlessly driving around town, I decided it might be a good idea to study at a diner. They always did it in movies—diners must be an inherently productive atmosphere. I drove to the end of Main Street and pulled into the warm-electric glow of Weatherford's only diner.

Fighting waves of nausea, I looked at the scene before me; the place was hopping. Every booth was filled with students guzzling coffee, buttering flapjacks, laughing and yelling, having a grand time. Maximum capacity laughed in my face. Even if a booth were to become available, I could never concentrate amid such chaos. I rolled down my window to a muffled roar of diner antics radiating from the building like invisible steam. Weatherford's anemic diner offerings would not suffice. I had to leave town.

I drove west through the town's dilapidated outskirts before reaching a two-lane highway quickly delivering me from familiarity. After several miles passed, I noticed that I-40 was running parallel to the road I was on. Wait a minute, if that's I-40 . . . . Slowing down, I flipped on my hi-beams to get a better look at an approaching sign that was severely sun-faded. A weight instantly dissolved from my shoulders as the replicating numbers I hoped for illuminated the night with a haunting presence—commanding authority to all who pass. In some twist of irony or fate, I had found myself on Route 66, The Mother Road.

I felt an immediate connection to the road that was indescribably organic, pure. America's most vital artery was pulsing against my tires, reverberating through the steering wheel and into my hands. It was alive, simultaneously comforting and haunting. For a brief moment, I felt the presence of all who have traveled the road before me. This road was like no other I had ever been on; it was magic.

My joyous elation soon turned to anger and gradually tapered into frustration. I grew up on my mother's childhood tales of Route 66, when the paint was fresh and the signs gave off a lacquered sheen. Their annual two-lane pilgrimage from Oklahoma to California makes up a large portion of our family's oral history.

Route 66 was the place Americans came to shake winter's dust from their boots, to experience an unknown thrill of the open road. Somewhere down the line, these common experiences evolved from family lore into thick slices of pure Americana.

Few domestic images stir emotion like a Dad's sun-tanned arm hanging out the window of a Plymouth wagon, hauling his nuclear family through the westbound glory of Route 66. Every few miles produced new roadside attractions, fanciful souvenir stands and cozy motels beckoning drivers with resplendent luminance and neon wonder. Everything on Route 66 was linked by a perpetual stream of diners, ready to meet the needs of any road-worn traveler. Diners were the cohesive binding that turned a 2400-mile stretch of asphalt into America's Main Street.

How had I lived in Weatherford for months without realizing that Route 66 passed through her heart? I thought the Mother Road had been destroyed under the iron fist of progress, leaving few drivable portions left. My lack of knowledge was disappointing. I had only heard about the romantic mystique of Route 66, never experiencing it for myself. The time was nigh.

Without realizing twenty minutes had passed, I saw the dull glow of a town begin to diffuse on the horizon. I drove toward the glow and found myself on Main Street of Clinton, Oklahoma. I had never been to Clinton before, yet something ahead was pulling me toward it with magnetic force. Like a robot on autopilot, I turned into a parking spot, killed the engine and blankly stared at the building in front of me.

A large metal sign with faded paint read: "Pop Hick's Restaurant." A Route 66 shield hung below it on a smoke-stained window. I was incredulous; had Route 66 sensed my desperation and led me to one of her own diners? Dazedly approaching the front door, I glanced at my watch; it was after midnight. I reached for the door expecting to find a dead bolt foiling yet another plan.

The overwhelming aroma of toast, bacon and Marlboro smoke washed across my face as the door swung open, spilling a small square of light onto the sidewalk. I stepped inside to a woven melody of disjointed conversation and clanking dishes that hung in the air below a thick cloud of cigarette smoke. A woman in classic waitress whites with a coffee pot fused to her arm looked my way as she sat down a plate of eggs and bacon.

"Pardon me ma'am, what time do you close?"

"Honey, this is Pop Hick's, we ain't closed in sixty-three years, decaf or regular?"

"Regular," I replied as she pointed me toward the back of the room where I found an empty booth and slid in. Turning my coffee cup right side up, the friendly woman filled it with steaming, jet-black coffee.

"You need to see a menu, or you just drinkin' tonight?"

"Coffee for now, but I may want something later."

"Well you just lemme know sugar, don't be shy." She then disappeared through a maze of tables, dropping long ropes of coffee into each passing mug, never spilling a drop.

Pop Hick's was an open floor plan with tables at its center, surrounded by a string of booths framing the room's square shape. The front wall was made of long, glass windows, giving every seat in the house a perfect view of Route 66. To the right of the door was a yellowed cash register, on a lunch counter symmetrically balanced with vinyl-topped barstools.

The focal point of the room was a long family-style table surrounded by chairs. Everything sat upon a floor silently advertising the millions of shoes that have passed over its surface. Decades of scuffs blended into faded wear-patterns reminiscent of an old cattle trail.

If there was one thing Pop Hick's had, it was charm. Unlike new restaurants capitalizing on Route 66's well-established diner legacy through contrived efforts of pre-fabricated nostalgia, Pop Hick's was the real deal. Authenticity is hard to counterfeit and this place was dripping in it. Purely

American, mid-century grandeur emitted from the walls, lingering like an unseen presence.

I was amazed at the volume of customers cycling through the restaurant's tables in the hours after midnight. People stopped in to eat a bite or tell a few stories, while others sat quietly . . . happy to be in the company of others. Pop Hick's was like the community's kitchen table; everyone had a place and there was always someone to listen.

Though most of the patrons were regulars, there was a salting of outsiders like myself. Everyone who passed through the door was greeted with a smile, and given a good morning when they left. It felt familiar. It felt comfortable. It felt like home.

At around five in the morning, a steady flow of old timers made their way through the door, each taking a seat at the long table in front of the bar. They were a mixture of retired farmers and working-class types, salt-of-the-earth men who devoted their entire lives to hard, honest work. You could see it in their faces, each suntanned line a testament to life not wasted.

The table soon filled with a dozen men hunched over steaming mugs, mumbling greetings to one another. By the second cup of coffee, caffeine was violently coursing through their veins and roaring laughter filled Pop Hick's with a presence bigger than life itself. Burning Marlboros hung from the lip of each man as they exchanged fantastic stories across the table.

"Honey, are they being too loud? I can shutem up for ya if ya like." The waitress caught me staring in awe of the men's sacred breakfast ritual while refreshing my coffee.

"Oh no ma'am I'm just trying to catch one of those stories, I bet they've got some great ones!"

"They may be great, but ain't none of 'em true. You see that table they're sitting at, we call that the liar's table." She cupped her hand to her mouth like a megaphone and turned toward the men shouting: "That's the liar's table and every man sitting at it earned their place!" The table erupted in great laughter, each man relishing their public recognition.

Breaking dawn poured through the front window, washing everything in the orange calm of morning. My test was an hour away and I'd not even opened a book. I was going to fail, but for some reason didn't even care. I'd found inspiration rather than concentration; Pop Hick's was a place for artistic ventures like writing or drawing, not studying.

Pop Hick's became the late-night gathering place for a select group of friends and myself. We'd head over about three times a week, and it wasn't rare to find dawn's first light spilling onto our corner booth littered in books and a night's worth of empty creamers. I even learned to study at Pop Hick's. When the evening's electricity started to wane and conversation became exhausted, we'd open our books. It turned out to be the perfect place to study; my grades improved drastically.

Pop Hick's wasn't the best restaurant in the world, but it never claimed to be. Its area of expertise was consistency. Any time of day, you could walk in and sit down to a good meal. The coffee was always hot and fresh, had been for sixty-three years. In a world of constant change, Pop Hick's remained an unmovable testament to a simpler time in America, when strangers said hello to one another and families went on Sunday drives. In some great confusion, time had overlooked Pop Hick's while everything around it remained in a perpetual state of change.

Spring soon came to Oklahoma, bringing with it the end of my first year of college. We all met at Pop Hick's on our last night for a final hurrah before going separate ways for the summer break. We talked and drank coffee until I was the only one left, finishing my last cup just before dawn. I paid the tab, assured my waitress we would see her in the fall and walked out the door.

The weary light of morning had fallen onto 66 when I turned around to find my reflection in the long window staring at me. In a moment of bittersweet realization, I bid farewell to my first year of freedom on the other side of the door in an empty booth, left for all eternity.

Route 66 escorted me back to Weatherford, where I merged onto I-40 for the long drive back to Locust Grove, Oklahoma, my hometown.

It was a balmy August night and I had just gotten home from my summer job delivering pizzas when the phone rang. It was my best friend from college and there was a somber tone in his voice.

"Did you hear the news?" he asked.
"No. What's wrong?"
"It's gone."
"What are you talking ab . . . ?"

"Burned to the ground. Pop Hick's is gone."

My eyes filled with unexpected tears and I felt like someone had kicked me in the stomach.

Pop Hick's opened its doors in 1936 and burned to the ground in an electrical fire on August 2, 1999. It was the longest running restaurant in the history of the Mother Road, a true Route 66 institution. When most diners were dismissed as antiquated relics, left to crumble in the wake of the twenty-first century's monolithic superhighways, Pop Hick's stood true. It was a no compromise, old guard diner that remained relevant when others could not.

When I got back to college in the fall, my first order of business was driving down old 66 to pay my respects to Pop Hick's. The eternal finality didn't register until I stood in the spot where my car had been parked on that first night. Instead of long windows, there was a yawning void. No Route 66 sign, no warm glow, not even the wall. I was looking into the burned-out charcoal shell of what used to be Pop Hick's. A lump formed in my throat as I looked upon a pile of black ash where the liar's table once stood. Sixty-three years of history were forever lost to the flames of fate. While taking pictures of the rubble, I realized how fortunate I was to find Pop Hick's when I did, only eight months before her fall.

This August marks the tenth anniversary of the diner's passing. All that remains at 223 W. Gary Blvd. is a gray slab of concrete; an unmarked gravestone baring witness to a life lived well. I often think about Pop Hick's and can't help but notice the significant transformation America has endured in its absence. Is it a coincidence, or did the last shred of the good old days burn up with the vinyl booths and the liar's table? Would Pop Hick's recognize the world it left behind?

Pop Hick's is often hailed a Route 66 institution. While this may be the case, institutions are formal and structured—Pop Hick's was not. Pop Hick's was a runaway train burning up the night, doling generous portions of hospitality to all who asked. It was America's Kitchen and the doors never closed. It was a constant. It wrapped around you like a warm blanket.

Though a sixty-three year run may seem substantial, those seeking sanctuary from the fast-paced entanglement of modern life will forever miss Pop Hick's ephemeral legacy. It's always hard to see a favorite restaurant lost to the pages of history—even harder when its mother was Route 66.

This manuscript is an account of how Luke became a regular at Pop Hick's, the longest-running restaurant in the history of The Mother Road—an experience that grabbed him by the jugular, infecting him with an insatiable urge to become part of Route 66's legacy. Writing is all that Luke has ever wanted to do. In college, he was a staff writer and a weekly columnist for The *Southwestern*. An Oklahoma native, he breaks the monotony of his blue-collar career by banging out words on his 1967 Olympia typewriter in his basement every night. He is a freelance writer and an aspiring novelist.

Walter's Last Ride

Willy

The man had on a pressed shirt and Bermuda shorts. The boys wore surfer shirts like half the young men in America. The wife was hiding her face behind a pair of oversized sunglasses. The man saw Walter at the counter, strolled on over with ministerial authority.

"Say, is that your horse you got saddled outside?"

Walter said, "Yep."

"Well, maybe you ought to have that rifle placed somewhere else. I got kids around. Something like that is likely to get people upset. You know the danger of firearms."

Walter gave the tourist a once over. No doubt an out-of-stater, a guy from Omaha with his wife and kids. Probably driving around in a station wagon.

"Well, sir, maybe I should," said Walter. "I appreciate the advice."

The tourist had been expecting a different response. He said, "I didn't want to bring it up but I thought I should point it out."

"No problem, sir. I see how it might bother you," said Walter. "I'll be sure to keep that in mind in the future."

"The wrong things happen when people get a firearm in their hands, especially young children."

Walter wondered how long the tourist had been cooped in his car, preaching to his family as they drove along the interstate. He said, "Well, sir, you have a good day."

"I will. I will have a good day."

The man departed. Walter watched the family settle in a booth, the kids climbing all over, making noise.

The waitress brought his check, said, "Bunch of do-gooders."

An old gal, probably sick of her job, working hard just to get by. Walter liked those lines in her face. He hoped his had the same proportions of good heart and tough work.

"Don't know how to leave a person alone."

"Nope," replied Walter. "Times are different."

"Yeah, the heck they are. But you don't got to worry, Mr. Wright. I'm on your side. I read about you in the *Albuquerque Journal* this morning. They made you out as some kind of monster, shooting up those kids' car. Well, I got news for them. My sister lives over in Corrales. She knows the family. Says those boys are the worst juvenile delinquents that ever came to town. Last Fourth of

July, someone stole a dog from a house, did some bad things to it, so bad it had to be put down. I don't have to tell you what they did. And you can guess no arrests were made, but all the signs pointed to those two boys. My sister says if you come down to Corrales, they'll give you a parade. I'll tell anyone in here if they ask. You're a real hero."

"I'm in the paper?"

"Yes you are, hon. Front page. Got a picture of you too. Looks pretty dandy."

Walter sipped his coffee. "Hmmm."

"You okay?"

"I guess I sure am."

"You look a little pale."

"I got me some slow flowing blood."

"You just sit right there as long as you want. I don't want you passing out on me."

"I'm fine. Just a little tired."

"Let me get you some fresh water."

The waitress left for water. Walter put a two-dollar bill on the counter, went to the door. His legs were weak and his heart was beating hard in his chest. He sat down outside on a flower box, put his hands on his knees, took a breath. The sun squeezed under the brim of his hat blurred his vision. He blinked, his eyes watering up so much he felt just like he was looking through a bottle of Karo corn syrup.

"Goddamn, goddamn!" he mumbled.

A highway patrol passed in front of the diner. Walter wiped his face. The car went slow down the highway, going east.

The waitress came out the door with a paper cup full of water. "Here you go, hon. You drink that."

"Thanks."

"You want me to call your family? Maybe say I saw you up this way?"

"No. I'm good. Just a little banged up."

Walter climbed up on Lucky, clicked the horse to a start.

"Come on, old boy. You get going now. You keep it up."

"You be safe."

"Will do."

Lucky stumbled on a fault in the pavement. Walter fell forward in the saddle, came down on the reins. Lucky pulled up. The road was a jumble of images.

"Oh Jeez," said Walter. He licked his lips, kicked Lucky to a trot and they scattered down the highway. Walter knew if he turned, he'd see that waitress looking after him, worried.

"Goddamn, here we go," said Walter. "Son of a bitch."

The wind started to pick up as they came on Milan. There were trucks on the road at this hour, doing the long haul west, throwing up dust and bits of slurried highway. Walter adjusted his hat, kept Lucky on the shoulder on a tight line. He didn't like getting that close to the broken bottles and cans the public threw from their cars, so he held the reins tight to the left, ready to pull Lucky if he strayed over.

At noon, they came across a man riding the other side. It wasn't until Walter was right up on him that he recognized the face. A man who'd worked for Walter once, cutting sheep. An itinerant. They shared salutes, passed. No name. Just a man hard on his luck. Walter rolled a Bull Durham. The tobacco stuck to the seeping cuts in his palm. He gave Lucky the reins, moved back up on the shoulder, smoking his cigarette pinched between his thumb and his index finger.

The western sun danced, slid slowly down the sky. Walter kept his head down, the hat brim shielding his face. Lucky, his neck bent now, was going slow.

They came across a billboard two hours before nightfall. The sign advertised the Sands Hotel in Las Vegas, 490 miles to the west, a shiny promise for the Minnesotans who were beginning to make the long February drive a winter ritual. Just a year old, the billboard was already peeling and cracked. Behind it ran an arroyo, almost dry now. A bank running slowly downwards. A good place to water and graze Lucky out of the limit of headlights shooting down the highway. There was a fire pit littered with cans and old gin bottles by the creek side. A bundle of rusted clothes hangers were wired up as a grill.

Walter set Lucky to graze by the creek, chewed a stick of jerky.

The hoboes came down the road at sunset—three of them, walking briskly. A pair of crows, who, like all crows, had the habit of flying silent at nightfall, preceded them. The hoboes entered the camp sideways in regulation homeless fear. An older fellow in a dusted up hat, a bandana rolled under the lining. A young man with a beard, his clothes beaten up and torn. A mixed blood man with a face worn down by alcohol abuse.

The man in the dusted up hat said, "Excuse me, mister, I hope you don't mind if we settle down here with you. See, this is kind of like our camp for the time being."

Walter said, "Sure, come on over."

"Yeah, we're kind of staying here," added the young one. His voice went up in question as he spoke. Walter registered the type. A person not quite right, used to being kicked around. The mixed blood man observed Walter from under his hat, eyes puffy, mouth turned down. Silent.

"I'm Stan," offered the older man. "And this is Lou and Carl."

"Pleased to meet you."

"Yeah, we been setting up here a while now," said Lou. "A while now. A whole while now."

"I see that."

"We been working down the road as day labor. They're paying a buck fifty an hour," explained Stan. "And we get to work the hours we please. Mostly rough work in the afternoon. But we're keeping up."

"Well, that ain't bad money," agreed Walter.

"No, it ain't bad at all," replied Stan. "Keeps us in supplies."

Carl said, "Hard work."

"Yeah, that's what it is," said Stan.

Walter said, "Say, you boys got something to drink?"

"Maybe we do."

"I got me a little bourbon if you're thirsty."

"Well, that ain't real necessary," said Stan. He tapped his coat pocket. "We're all carrying. We're just damned lucky to get the work we got, a place to stay."

"Well, that's a bright spot," said Walter.

"Yes it is," agreed Lou, his whole face nodding, beard shaking. "Yes it is. Yes it is. Yes it is. Yes it is. Yes it is."

"Lou's been in electro-shock therapy over in Fort Worth. Sometimes he says things a few times," said Stan. "Don't mind him. It ain't a problem. You just got to listen twice."

"I sometimes do that too," said Walter. "Every now and then you got to say something twice."

"Yes you do," agreed Stan. Then, "Say, Carl, how about you set up the fire?"

The hoboes gathered sticks and debris from the creek. Carl lit the fire and set a couple of cans of stew on the edge of the flames. The men sat at the edge of the pit and drank. Walter figured their work wouldn't last long, maybe a couple of days, and then they'd be back to collecting bottles and sweeping sidewalks for a tenth of what they were making as day laborers. They weren't the types to work at anything for long.

"Say, Walter, where, where, where you say you were heading?" asked Lou when the comfort of alcohol was sitting on him.

Carl gave Lou a look. And Stan said, "Now Lou, you know you don't ask a man that. It ain't polite."

Lou nervously scratched his beard. Even though he was only twenty-three, there were lines of gray in it. "I didn't mean to be rude, mister," he said, the words pouring out quickly, his voice going up. "I was just trying to be friendly."

"Nothing wrong with being friendly," said Walter.

"No, nothing wrong with that," said Stan.

"So where you heading?" asked Lou again, then added a quick, nervous laugh.

Carl grimaced.

Stan gave Lou a kick. "Why don't you tell him about your electro-shock, Lou?" he demanded.

Lou frowned. "No, it ain't nothing. Ain't nothing."

"You got it right that time," said Stan. "It's none of our business where Walter's heading."

"I'm going south," said Walter. "Guess I figured I'd go that way for a while. Don't know how I'll get there."

Stan clicked his tongue, said, "Well, there you go."

"Mister, you want to try some of my wine?" asked Lou.

"No thanks. I think I'm pretty much done," Walter replied. His throat was hot from the bourbon. And the fire made him restless. A highway patrol might see the glow from the road. Soon enough the hoboes would start to thinking that camp was theirs. And Stan, used to being in charge, would see how far he could push Walter. Walter stood, shook out his trousers.

"You leaving us already?" wondered Stan.

"Checking on my horse."

Walter felt his stomach turn as he approached his horse. Lucky's left shoulder was trembling. And he was breathing heavy like the air was too thick.

"Goddamn, I'm sorry about that highway. It's busting you up." Walter put his hand on Lucky's neck. The old Appaloosa nuzzled him. "We do this and then we move on. Only a few miles left."

Stan was standing over Lucky's saddle, looking at the rifle when Walter returned. He saw Walter coming and stepped back quickly.

"Just looking at your piece, Walter," said Stan. "I ain't touching nothing. Just seeing what you got."

"I see that."

"You can check it if you like. I didn't touch nothing. Not a thing. Just looking."

Lou nodded and pulled his arms around his knees. Carl looked into the fire, sucked a sunburned lip.

"Something wrong, Walter?"

"Nope."

"It's plenty dark right now. Not a good time to be getting out."

"Well, the way I see it is that I don't sleep so much nowadays," said Walter. "And this fire's got my horse a little shaken up. So I'm going down the highway a bit. Find a place a little calmer. Maybe look at the stars."

"Well, that's your right, mister. It sure is your right," agreed Stan.

The hoboes watched Walter saddle his horse, talking low. Drinking.

When Walter had Lucky all tacked up, Stan said, "About that bourbon, mister. You think you might want to leave us the bottle?"

The bottle was by the fire, half-empty. The hoboes had already taken a few chugs from it.

Probably when Walter was checking on his horse. Maybe the reason Stan looked nervous when Walter came back to the fire.

"It's all yours."

"Well damn, that's awfully nice of you, mister," said Stan.

"My pleasure."

Walter led Lucky up to the highway. He walked ahead of the Appaloosa, the reins loose in his hands. Two miles up the road, he found a drive. The farm was unlit. Most likely a place for sale. It would be going full run otherwise. The fencing along the drive was a good ten feet from the road. Walter found a spot that looked as soft as could be expected. He pulled Lucky's saddle to the dirt, dropped off the bridle.

"Hell, I'm sorry about the move."

Lucky snuffled the grass. Sighed.

Walter looked up at the New Mexico sky. It was bristling with stars. He thought of his last night with Sarah Begay. He was twenty-five years old. Fifty years ago now. He and Sarah were in a prohibition hotel across the state line.

"I thought you wouldn't want me," confessed Sarah as they lay together in the room. She had her face in Walter's chest, was speaking to his heart.

Walter was quiet, unsure what to say. He wanted to hold Sarah to him and never release her. He knew it was selfish even then, but he couldn't remove the thought from his mind. Holding her forever.

"I waited in Santa Fe, took a job in a motel."

"I heard from dad you might be up there."

"I had to quit when I started to show."

"You didn't write."

"No."

Walter nodded. He remembered the two postcards she had sent him while he was in Albuquerque, a couple of black and white photographs of the badlands, a penny stamp attached to each. A childish scrawl of which Walter suspected she was painfully ashamed. No, Sarah wouldn't write. It was a mechanism that had failed on her.

Walter elongated himself against her. His face drawn. Still. His eyes closed. He couldn't look at her. She, smooth, next to him, her earthy smell filling him.

"What's her name?" said Walter slowly, gauging his reaction, holding it in. No anger. Just pain.

"Celia."

"And who took her?"

"A married couple from Los Angeles. They drove all the way out here for her. It was all arranged."

"They paid you?"

"It was all legal. Drawn up. She was Mexican. He was a white man."

Walter felt his heart slip. He thought of saying, "Why didn't you call me?" But it would be useless. What good would it be to ask? The act was done.

"I thought you wouldn't want me."

Walter stood. He went to the window. The loss welling up, making his skin hot. "You didn't wait for me when I went to Albuquerque."

Sarah brushed the rough cotton sheets over her belly. She glanced at Walter. "I was just speaking, saying things. I didn't mean it to hurt you. You weren't there, Walter. You never came."

"To your aunt's house?"

"I couldn't stay there."

Sarah sleeping in the same bed with her two cousins. A few yards of cloth a year to make dresses. Work for handouts. Maybe some nice clothes from the mission.

Walter looked at his horse. Lucky was only a few feet away from him, his breathing deep, regular. Walter put his arms around the horse, said, "Amigo."

He imagined he was holding Sarah.

"I didn't come for you," said Walter to Lucky, "because you were an Indian. And I was scared, so goddamned scared of doing this."

Sarah didn't move from Walter's grasp. It was not a secret. She knew it was to be that way. Walter as he stood on the mining camp, looking at her.

Walter's father looking at her; Walter's father who said to Walter, "She's going to be a pretty one."

Walter fell asleep. Next to him, Lucky sleeping. A warm night turning cold.

Walter woke with a startled breath. A diesel truck, its transmission grinding, blasted by on the highway. Walter peered at the quiet Lucky. The Appaloosa was on his side, his neck turned to the road, ears forward, waiting. Behind him, a man standing, quiet, arms around his chest. Walter felt his stomach turn. He brushed his face, blinked, and forced his eyes to focus.

"Is that you, Carl?"

"Yep."

"Why you following me?"

"I don't know. I just thought maybe . . . well, I thought something."

"What were you thinking, Carl?"

Carl had his hat in his left hand, was squeezing it tightly.

"I know who you are," said Carl.

"You been reading about me in the paper?"

"No, I'm saying I seen you before."

"Okay."

"Yeah, you know, a long time ago."

"Is that so?"

"I was just a kid. Not real old. But I remember."

Walter waited. They could go a long time talking like this. Carl fishing at his point. Letting the conversation build slow, Navaho style. Not saying what was on his mind, getting to the point slow and courteous.

"Mr. Wright, sir, I know the story about how your father got that horse."

"Well, maybe you do. I expect a few people do."

"How he paid half of what he should've."

"There were some who said that," agreed Walter.

The two men regarded each other. It took Walter some time before he figured it out, then said, "You're from Rock Point."

"I am."

"A good place."

"I saw you ride in the rodeo when I was a kid. You were the best damned cowboy I ever saw."

"Maybe that day I was. I wasn't really a good cowboy on most days."

"But everyone said it was all your horse."
"I think it was."
"Yeah, I think it was too."

Walter looked again at Carl's hat all bundled up. Carl was swaying a little. Drunk.

"Yeah," said Carl. "Yeah, just wanted to tell you that. Everyone said you had a big heart."

Walter took a breath. The heart he used to have, the kind that gives life. His arms were like bars. He could laugh and everyone around him would set off in laughter. The heart he used to have. It was big shouldered and wonderful mean.

"I appreciate it, Carl."

"You know, I ain't too good now, Mr. Wright. Things were better for me back then. I just thought I'd let you know I remembered seeing you ride. You had a helluva seat. And the best damned horse ever bred."

Walter nodded.

"I know my dad paid half the price for the horse. We weren't proud of it. But he had to pick up other things."

Things. Meaning Mary Begay. But Walter was unable to say it. And Carl knew anyways, him being from Rock Point. Mary, who came with the horse because that was the week they killed her father. Government agents shooting Navaho. 1890. The big circus horse getting on its knees, offering its front right hoof to be shaken by the men left living. Mary, Sarah's Mother, who had been living on boiled grass and clay. And no family to feed her well. Half price for the horse. And then Mary. To keep the house.

"I know."

"Enough said."

"Mr. Wright, what Stan said back there at the camp about us making a buck fifty an hour. You know, he was lying. It was Stan that made the buck fifty. We all got four bits each, doing odd jobs. Then Stan collected our money. Said three drunks were worth one man's labor."

"You need money, Carl?"

"Naw. I was just saying we ain't as set up as Stan was making out. When you left, there was talk about maybe, you know, coming and getting something off of you. So I came up first, to make sure you were okay . . . in case Stan got ideas. He ain't a bad guy. But sometimes he takes things a little farther than they should go."

"Like playing with my rifle."

"That's Stan."

"So you're saying I should push on."

"I guess I am."

Walter pulled his sleeping roll around his shoulders.

"My horse is damned beat out."

"I know. But I'm not kidding about Stan. And Lou'll do whatever Stan asks. He can't help it. He's tied to Stan. And Stan knows it."

"What about you, Carl?"

"I ain't a fighter, Mr. Wright. I never was. I'm no good at it. I'll help you saddle the horse, and then you better move on."

"Well, shit."

"That's about how it is, Mr. Wright."

Lucky took the saddling with the resignation of a tired horse. Good old Lucky. The two men worked quickly in the moonlight. Walter brushing down, Carl setting the saddle pad. Walter put on Lucky's bridle, worked the bit gently into his soft mouth. Carl had Lucky saddled with three good pulls on the cinch. Walter climbed up on the horse's back. He sat, rolled himself a cigarette.

"Carl, where are they waiting for me?"

"Pard me, Mr. Wright?"

"Stan sent you up front."

Carl studied his hands. Sighed. "He's got a transistor radio. Heard about you on the reports. They're looking for you in the four corner states."

"What was your job?"

"I was to get the rifle."

"Then what?"

"We weren't going to hurt you, Mr. Wright. Honest. But we figured you had some money. Man riding around on a horse like that. You know, what they said on the news . . . ."

Walter pulled his rifle from the saddle. "Here, Carl, you take it. I don't have a need for it anymore. If Stan asks, you tell him you got the rifle and I got the horse."

"Jesus, Mr. Wright. I don't need a rifle. Folks see me with it they'll know it ain't mine."

Walter rolled forward in the saddle, extracted his wallet.

"And there's a hundred dollars there, Carl. You take that too. I figure we're even. You can buy a used car. Maybe get drunk for a month. Or get down to New Orleans and meet a gal. Those two, Carl, they'll bring you down."

"Jesus Christ, I know that."

"Where are they waiting, Carl?"

"They're lying up for you at the end of the road."

"I'll see you later."

Walter clicked Lucky to a walk. The old horse moved forward slowly. Walter turned, saw Carl squatting on the ground, the rifle across his knees. Carl raised his hat in salute, then brought it down quick, worried. Walter brought the gelding up to a trot.

Stan and Lou were waiting at the end of the road. Walter thought they looked like a couple of cutout dolls, waving their arms like that. And then he saw the plan. They were going to grab the reins or maybe get a hand on Lucky's bridle as he came up. An old trick every farm hand knew. A good way to get a horse that's lost its rider.

Stan called, "Hold up, hold up there, Walter. Where you going?"

Walter dug into Lucky's flank and gave the Appaloosa his rein.

"Get up."

"Hey, wait a minute . . . ."

Stan grabbed for the halter, but horse and rider were moving faster than he'd expected. He clawed at Lucky's hindquarters, slipped. Lucky's hock jammed Stan's wrist into his chest, sent the drunk spinning to the road top. Lou grabbed Walter's leg, hung on, his arm pinched between stirrup leather and the girth. He was not a horseman and had no clue as to what he had done. Lucky kept his stride, his momentum building. The force wrenched Lou from the ground, once, twice, dislocated his shoulder. The young man yelped, released, fell to the roadside.

"Oh Jesus, Jesus, Jesus," cried Lou.

Walter, head down, steered Lucky over on the highway.

"You get the hell back here, Walter Wright," shouted Stan.

"Jesus, Jesus, Jesus," shouted Lou.

Walter put his head down, brought Lucky up to a gallop.

A half mile down the road, the cries died down.

"Goddamn, amigo, this is a night," Walter told his horse.

Lucky plodded on. Faithful Lucky, who gave himself completely to Walter.

Dawn. Walter brushed Lucky's broad back, checked his hooves, picked carefully around the steel shoes, looking for signs of stress. The hooves were fine. Meaning the wear was further up, joint resting on joint, tendons tight and overworked.

"Goddamn, I'm sorry about this, amigo."

Lucky snorted, and his bottom lip trembled. There was no coffee, and Walter moved thickly. His hip hurt, a dull, grinding pain. He dragged a leg behind him, hoped he'd warm up soon, get things moving. Walter found a handful of oats at the bottom of his saddlebags. Lucky's soft mouth gently rustled the grain off the earth as Walter saddled him.

"We're almost there, amigo," said Walter. "And then we take a rest."

The highway was alive with diesel trucks rolling west. Horse and rider took a slow start. The wind blew in their faces, setting Walter's teeth to chatter. Lucky kept his head down, ears turned out.

They entered Thoreau. Barely a few homes. A stop on the interstate. Walter talked to a man out for a walk with his dog, asked for the whereabouts of the ranch. The man said it was up the highway, 66 to 371 towards Smith Lake. Couple of miles. Walter would see the mailbox, next to it a broken down truck painted blue. Walter thanked the man, gave Lucky a click. The dog barked until horse and rider were a quarter of a mile along, announcing their passage.

Just one truck passed on the highway north. A weekday. Men working the ranches, the inevitable pull of the coming winter.

Lucky was striding now, head pumping, sensing they would soon stop, thinking of alfalfa and grain. Walter rolled a Bull Durham. The nicotine laid bitter on his lips. He coughed, the nighttime phlegm still on his throat. Walter felt lightheaded. He gave Lucky the reins.

The broken down blue truck was there as the man had explained. Walter tapped Lucky on the right flank. The Appaloosa followed the lead, down the drive, his pace quickening, almost to a trot. Walter made a farmer's note to himself as they went down the lane. A farm in decline. Dry farming. Too much for the residents to handle. The touch of a man no longer there. The slow tug of poverty.

The state trooper was waiting in his patrol car at the edge of the house. He'd arrived in a load of dust, pulling a horse trailer behind his car. He was off duty for the weekend but still wore his uniform because those were his orders. He saw the old cowboy coming and stayed in his vehicle.

Walter pulled Lucky to a halt. Sat.

Sarah's daughter from her second husband came out on the porch. Diane, a tall woman, wavy hair, a pinched face, favoring her father's basque blood.

Walter hitched Lucky on the porch.

"I think you're going to be arrested, Walter," Diane pointed out. She nodded towards the patrol car.

"I figured as much."

Diane leaned over the porch, touched the star on Lucky's forehead. The Appaloosa moved his head in, waited for a scratch.

"Mom's inside."

Sarah was at a card table, a pair of oversized glasses on her nose, shelling a pound of beans.

"Walter, I heard you were coming."

Walter pulled a chair from under the table. It scraped across the floor, and Sarah turned to it. Walter registered the unfocused look. The wall of cataracts. The glasses on her nose as if to say she wasn't really blind.

"I don't see so good now, Walter," she announced.

Sarah put her hand to her face. Removed her glasses. Though her eyes were no good, she was looking at Walter.

Silence. Each waiting for the other to speak.

Then, Walter said, "I don't think so good nowadays. I'm forgetting things. I look around and everything is unfamiliar. And I'm scared half the damned time. I live in the past. The old stuff looks sharper and more alive. I get worried because you get remembered for not doing things right."

Sarah blinked, pushed her glasses up the ridge of her nose.

Walter pushed his hat across the table. From the door, he could feel the state trooper looking at him, gauging when he should come in.

"I never was good with showing how I felt."

"No, Walter, you weren't at that."

If Sarah's eyes were still good, she would have seen that Walter was crying. Slow, cautious tears, the kind that get caught in a man's eyes, never falling. She saw instead the day Walter rode away. Sarah was on the steps of the mission. She was twenty-nine. Her husband, a tall man from the reservation, was next to her.

He was stooped from work in the mines, twenty years her elder. Walter turned off the path to the mission and ran across the yard. Sarah's eyes followed him as he took his horse to a gallop. She saw Walter's wide brimmed hat, the worn out McClellan saddle, the chaps with the swirl of white stars painted on the bells, the sturdy shoulders hunched forward in anguish. Walter, the father of her first daughter.

E. G. Willy is a West Coast educator and writer whose works have appeared in anthologies and publications in the US, Canada, and Great Britain. His poetry and spoken word pieces have aired on public and college radio shows around the country.

Conelrad in the Wigwam

Jimmy J. Pack Jr.

My Route 66 travel partner, Joel Bukiewicz, and I arrive at the Wigwam Motel in Holbrook, Arizona, July 2001. This is one of three Wigwam Villages remaining in the United States. The first Wigwam Village was built in Horse Cave, Kentucky by Frank A. Redford, which featured one large central teepee building surrounded by six smaller teepee guestrooms. Four years later, Redford built another in Cave City, Kentucky, this time with a larger central teepee housing a restaurant and gift shop surrounded by fifteen smaller teepee guestrooms. In 1940, two more popped up, one in Bessemer, Alabama, with fifteen guestroom teepees and the other in Orlando, Florida—double the size of the previous Wigwam Villages, thirty-one guestroom teepees. Our Wigwam Village is number six, Holbrook, built by a local motelier Charles E. Lewis, in 1950. The seventh one was built in Rialto, California around 1949, also by Redford, for himself.

When the Holbrook motel rooms were built, there was no such concept as "The Franchise," so Lewis agreed to install coin-operated radios—ten-cents for a half-hour of music—and send all the money to Redford as a payment for letting him use the Wigwam design.

I can already tell I'm going to love Holbrook. Our Wigwam Village is a neatly planned rectangle formation with vintage cars planted around the parking lot and in front of the motel office. I grab two keys and we set-up camp. Inside are two beds, a rustic nightstand made of thick sticks with the bark intact, shellacked for protection, next to each bed. A bathroom is tucked under the edge of the teepee between our beds. I start the air conditioner as Joel opens the door and a side window and takes off his shoes.

"I'm hungry, man," says Joel who grabs the Route 66 Dining and Lodging Guide, put out by the National Historic Route 66 Federation, and within seconds chooses a place to eat.

"The Butterfield Stage Company. Right next door. I don't know why but I can go for a steak."

"You're home on the range," I say, pulling out my camera to take a few photos outside.

"I'm going to shower and we'll head over. Is that all right with you?"

"Sounds good."

I skulk around the parking lot taking as many photos as I have rolls of film to fill. I peek into some of the vintage cars and notice the old radios—all AM stations. They remind me of my old man's LeMans that he loved—speeding around the Connecticut interstates blasting news radio, listening for stock tips. When there were thunderstorms, you could hear the lightning break static in the broadcast. And just like his radio, there are two strange looking triangles between the numbers of six and seven, and twelve and fourteen.

The Conelrad Stations were used as warnings—Americans, dive under your desks or hide in your basements and showers, the nuclear bombs from The Commies are coming. It reminds me of the old Emergency Broadcast System test screen that interrupted my TV shows when I was a kid. No one ever explained to me what they were.

For a while, when I was a little kid, I thought someone on TV knew if we were going to have a fire in the house, so they were televised fire drills for people's homes. When I got older, I realized the map of Connecticut broken up into three different color-coded areas had little to do with my house and more to do with something much bigger than losing my Duran Duran cassette tapes, homework and clothes in a fire. No, it was all a national party whistle to let you know you were going to be incinerated in a matter of minutes.

That's when my anxiety went from the stage of worrying about dying as a child—to worrying about being killed by the world in the middle of puberty in a quick, semi-painless flash of fused atoms or, worse, to suffer the loss of water in my body and bloody sores scabbing up and getting wider as the radiation pulls all my hair out and forces every vapor of acid out of my stomach and behind.

Conelrad Stations—pretty much a joke considering a GPS tracker can find me via satellite within a few feet of accuracy, and you don't need to worry about inches, feet or a few miles when you've got the A-bomb ready to be jammed in your skull. So, it's fitting that this Wigwam Village, Number six, is one of only three surviving teepee motels. To anyone driving by them in a world of Super 8s and Hampton Inns, these giant triangles are no sign of welcome. They're not even motels—they're relics. An archaic way of sleeping like trying to nap in a tree, or making an empty bear cave your home for the night. Where are the telephones? The internet? The plastic headboards nailed to the walls and in-room cable movies for $12.99 a rental?

This is an experience—this is something you do. Sure, concrete teepees are a gimmick, but how often do you get to sleep in one? You can't hear your neighbors through the walls or at your door as they drunkenly walk by after enjoying a few watered down Jack and Diets from the dust bar downstairs with the large-screen projector TV and ripped pleather seats. You're cocooned in this wigwam, which is a stress reliever from the tensions and anxiety emanating from the Mother Road. I know I need it . . . but Joel needs a steak.

Still, as I look from the inside of the car over to our Wigwam, I can't help but think about how safe this area would be from a nuclear attack. Who would want to bomb a teepee? The anxiety of being so far away from home needs to be quelled with a dinner—a juicy steak and a few drinks from Butterfield Stage Company and I think everything will be all right.

Jimmy J. Pack Jr. is a writer living in Philadelphia. Pennsylvania. He received his MA in Creative Writing from Temple University and has had his writing published in *The Helix, Just a Moment, Café 84, Howling Dog Magazine, Pangolin Papers, Mobius, The Berkeley Fiction Review* and *Route 66 Magazine*. He teaches writing at The Pennsylvania State University—Abington.

A Route 66er since his first trip down the Mother Road in 2001, he also runs a Web site of Road-Side American photography at rt66photos.com. Anyone interested can email him at jimmyjpackjr1@mac.com, or visit his website at www.jimmyjpackjr.com.

Homecoming

Linda Neal Reising

How awkward
to be standing at a salad bar
in the truck stop café
of a one-horse, Route 66 town,
where you grew up too fast
too many years ago to count,
and where you think no one's alive
who'll remember you,
and besides, you have half the hair
and twice the you,
and everyone who could move, did,
to Broken Arrow or Broken Bow,
ordinary places with John Wayne names,
and no one knows
about the poems you write,
the ones about him,
the wrongs he committed against you,
when you were too innocent to know

Lost On Route 66

that *no* should have meant *no*,
but you had no phrase
for it back then, only silence
that you've kept until now
at this salad bar, coleslaw spoon
mid-air, and he is there,
asking how you are,
and you smile one more time,
and say *fine*, lower the spoon,
and fork a pickled beet,
lift it bleeding onto your plate.

Arizona Highways

Linda Neal Reising

Blue. Brown. Black and white. Gray. Was that a Chevy? The cars going by on the highway were only colors to him. He had almost no notion of make or model. Inside the last one, he could see a woman driver, and he thought she waved at him. Foster didn't return the greeting. She was probably just making fun of him anyway. He'd had some troubles in the past with people on the Route. A group of boys in a rusty rattletrap had chucked hedge apples at him as he sat in his metal lawn chair. Most had splattered against the house, breaking open like green brains.

That was why he'd posted the "No Trespassing" and "Keep Out" signs all over the side of his gray shingled house and along the old fence posts bordering his property. Or had he posted the warnings before the teenagers hurled the wrinkled missiles? He couldn't remember, but he knew he hated them, hated all of them for their ignorance, zooming along as if they could outrun the inevitable.

Foster McGee knew about the inevitable. From the time he was sixteen until he retired at sixty-five, fourteen years ago, he had been a stone carver. Once or twice, he had been commissioned to complete a project for a library or a park, but day after day, his livelihood came from the inevitable. He was a carver of tombstones.

When Foster first started his apprenticeship with an uncle who suffered from arthritis, the boy had thought of himself as an artist. Very gently, he would caress the stone, as if taming it, calming it before driving the first blow. He became adept not only at forming precise letters but also at relief carvings of angels, lilies, and Jesus portraits with light beams radiating from his robes.

He could remember precisely when the futility of his art, in fact of all human endeavors, finally settled over him like a pall or a mist in a sunless valley. Foster had been carving stones for eighteen years when the flu epidemic swept the country like a grassfire that couldn't be contained. People could only stand by and see their loved ones burning with fever. They were helpless as the illness leapt from person to person like airborne sparks, until only ashes remained.

The years of 1918 and 1919 were prosperous ones for Foster McGee, but as he carved, sometimes into the night to keep up with the demand, he found himself becoming resentful, scoffing at the messages he himself wrote in stone: In God's arms now. An angel gone home to heaven.

What kind of God would make babies suffer? Would rip mothers away from their children, children still too young to remember her face? No, there was no God. Foster McGee was sure of that. And it was this revelation that had changed him, shut him off from those who still tried to find some hope, something to believe in.

This particular morning, then, Foster sat in his rusty yellow lawn chair and scowled at the traffic of Route 66. He'd already had his breakfast, the same one he had every morning, two eggs with yokes soft enough to be sopped up by toast and a glass of buttermilk. Now he was settling down to read the daily newspaper and *Arizona Highways*, both delivered to his mailbox, which sported a "Beware of Dog" sign on its post, although he hadn't owned a dog in twelve years.

From force of habit, Foster always turned to the obituaries first, although he'd lost contact with everyone except his nephew, who brought him groceries a couple times a month. He didn't even own a car that ran. Honeysuckle vines and blackberry brambles overgrew his old Buick. Each year it sank deeper into the canopy of foliage until the bumpers and top peeked out like the remnants of some lost Incan temple in a Peruvian jungle. Isolated, he still checked the deaths. Sometimes he recognized a family name, but he did not feel any emotion. It was the same as reading the weather forecast, although much more predictable.

After the obituaries, he always turned back to the front page and read every column of every page, even if the articles dealt with child rearing or women's intimate health problems, topics he had absolutely no use for. On this morning, he murmured aloud, "Damn fools!" as he read about President Kennedy's ongoing dispute with Castro. "Just trying to show who has the biggest balls." Foster talked to himself regularly, pleased that there was no one to argue with his viewpoint.

He read article after article—horoscopes that he found laughable, reviews of movies he'd never see, letters to the editor about local issues he didn't understand. Finally, after he'd even skimmed the grocery store ads and the classifieds, he carefully folded the pages up, a butterfly being returned to its cocoon. He placed it at his feet, but later he'd add it to the stack behind his cast iron wood stove. By winter, he'd have months of words to burn.

Next, he opened the latest issue of *Arizona Highways*. This was his only weakness, his sole indulgence. Other men battled the bottle or fell under the spell of women or gambling. But Foster was addicted to *Arizona Highways*.

It all started one Saturday when James, his nephew, brought over a crate of items that Nell, his wife, intended to give to the Salvation Army. James, however, had suggested they let Foster look first. The old man had grumbled something about feeling like a bum digging through a trashcan, but he did pull out a blanket that looked like the satin trim had been chewed by a dog, a faded flannel shirt, a collection of unused bumper stickers from places he'd never visited, and a stack of *Arizona Highways*.

Foster was a little disturbed to find out later that Nell or one of her three grandchildren had pulled or snipped out many of the pages. He could only guess by reading the accompanying article what the Tucson sunsets or the Flagstaff snowcaps had looked like in the pictures, now that only a few tattered remains stuck to the binding.

He found the address to subscribe and sent in his money, wrapped inside a piece of paper, along with a note containing his address. As time went by, Foster feared that someone in a mailroom along the way had opened the envelope and stolen his money. Hadn't the magazine requested that cash not be sent? But eventually the periodicals started rolling in as steadily as the traffic outside his house.

Saguaros. Those were his favorites, big as trees with arms like bragging muscle men. Foster made frames for several different shots—saguaro in bloom, saguaro in sunlight, saguaro at sunset. He dreamed of someday going there in the same way that ordinary housewives dream of making love to movie stars.

On this particular day, Foster spent the entire morning reading first the newspaper and then the magazine. Only when his stomach protested did he pull himself up with a huff and go inside to open a can of potted meat, which he slapped between some pieces of cold cornbread left over from the night before. He was careful to wash his plate out afterwards because last year, when he'd gotten a little lax about his dishwashing, the ants had just about carted off the kitchen.

Now the afternoon loomed before him like a shadow. Each day, weather permitting, he sat outside carving, not in stone but in wood from trees he hacked down around his house or in driftwood that James picked up for him when the river was low. Foster had lost faith in the saving power of art years before, but he couldn't stop carving, like a priest who hears confessions and gives absolution in the name of the Father, the Son, and the Holy Spirit, although he's not sure he believes in even one, let alone the Trinity.

Foster did not know why he carved what he did. In fact, he was really quite embarrassed by the finished pieces, but he couldn't bear to throw them away or stuff them into the glowing mouth of the iron stove. Instead, he hid them within boxes stacked inside a closet in the hallway. Mummified inside the closet were dragons, covered with tiny intricate scales, rearing up and shooting fire from flaring nostrils or lips. Sumptuous goddesses with delicate arms and fingers, wearing gowns too filmy to be poplar. Raging stallions, swatting bears, fleeing elk.

Once done, Foster McGee put them away and did not look at them again. These beings and creatures he created would go on living long after he was dust. He told himself he should destroy them, but he couldn't bring himself to do so, and he couldn't stop creating them. The only solution was to hide them away, bound in his closet like abused children.

* * *

Rhonda Bell was low on gas and even lower on money. She steered the Studebaker to the side of the road. She opened her leather purse, tooled like a saddle, and felt inside for any loose change. She pulled out a handful of tattered Kleenex and fifty-seven cents.

"Damn it."

She had been driving since four in the morning when she stole the car from her stepfather's garage, Stanley's Fix It Fast, where it was waiting retrieval by its owner. Rhonda had stopped long enough to fill up the tank and grab snacks, whose wrappers littered the floorboard. Now the money she'd taken out of her mother's purse and the smiling pig cookie jar in the kitchen was almost gone.

With a quick look around to see if anyone was coming, she guided the car off the edge of the highway and into a small grove of trees. Warily, Rhonda glanced into the rearview mirror to see if anyone was coming, but all she saw were her own eyes, brown with an orange tint, like a tabby cat. She flipped back the long red braid that lay across her chest before shutting off the motor and dropping the keys into her purse.

Even though it was late in the afternoon when she saw the gray house, plastered with its armor of unwelcoming signs, the sun was still warm, and the shirt she wore, with "Stanley" embroidered in a little circle over her left breast was wet and clinging. Noiselessly, she held up the barbed wire and crawled through the fence. The old man sitting outside was bent over. At first, Rhonda thought he might he dozing, but then she saw his hands moving, woodchips flying. He was whittling something. That meant he'd be armed, but so was she.

So intense was his concentration or perhaps his hearing so poor, that he did not notice her, did not look up, until she said sweetly, "Sir?"

The old man started with a "What?"

"I didn't mean to scare you."

She could see his face go red like someone caught.

"Can't you read? You think all these signs are up just to make the place look pretty?"

"No, sir." Rhonda tried to capture the expression that had always fooled her parents and teachers before they learned to read her face and the truth that lay beneath.

"Well, then, why are you here?" She could hear his voice softening.

"I ran out of gas back on the highway, and I was wondering if I could use your phone."

"I don't have a phone, and I don't have any gasoline either. I guess you're out of luck."

Rhonda sighed and hung her head in a show of disappointment. Mentally, she was wondering if she could wrestle the tool from the old man's gnarled fingers. Surely she was stronger. But now she could see that there was no need. He added the blade to his collection, housed inside a long leather pouch that rolled into a bundle and tied with rawhide strings. Whatever he'd been working on, he stuck inside the chest of his shirt.

"Thank you anyway. Could you tell me how far it is to the next house?" She kept her eyes lowered and drew circles in the dust with the toe of her cowboy boot.

"About a mile. You can't miss it."

Rhonda turned as if to go, but wheeled back around. "I hate to trouble you again, but it's awfully hot. Do you think I could have a drink of water?"

The old coot was sizing her up. She tried to soften her features as much as possible and let her braid fall to the front. Why hadn't she loosened it before approaching the old guy? There was something about long hair that could get to a man, even an old fossil like this one.

"Oh, all right." It took some effort for him to pull himself from the chair. "You stay here, and I'll bring it out."

As soon as he rounded the side of the house, she followed. At first, Rhonda was startled by what she saw. Unlike the front, this side was decorated with hubcaps and license plates, arranged in daisy patterns. Obviously, these items had been scavenged from along the highway, or perhaps some had even rolled into his yard, trespassing on his holy ground. So he'd crucified them, nailed them as a warning, like a hunter stretches a coyote carcass across a fence post.

Quickly, Rhonda unsnapped her purse and eased the gun out, just as he turned around to say, "I thought I told you . . . ." His forehead fell to wrinkles and then his whole body sagged.

"You told me what, old man? I don't like being told where I can go or what I can do." She felt the gun make contact with his ribs. "Is anyone else home?"

"I live alone."

Rhonda snorted. "I wonder why? You seem like such a loving kind of guy. Open the door."

She followed him inside and looked around at the faded linoleum, sagging paper, and antiquated appliances. Why, out of all the places on Route 66, did she have to run low on gas here, near this hermit's house? But sometimes those were the ones with cash hidden away. Hadn't old man

Gradey, who lived on the outskirts of town, planted his money in the garden? He'd been dead nearly two years when some distant cousin who'd inherited the place plowed up a fortune in a row of mayonnaise jars.

"Sit down. You weren't lying about the phone, were you?"

"No, I don't have one. Who would I call?"

"Right about now, I'd say the police might be a good choice." Rhonda laughed hard, expressing more amusement than she felt. She pulled a dishtowel, made from a flour sack, from a rod beside the sink. After sticking the gun into her waistband, she quickly tied the old man's wrists together behind the rungs of the wooden chair she had pushed him into. "You just sit tight while I look around."

Foster McGee knew he'd made what could prove to be a fatal error when he heard the girl's footsteps behind him. She'd looked so sweet, helpless. But the gun wasn't entirely a surprise. He's always figured someone from the Route would kill him, but he just didn't expect it to be a red-haired female.

Now here he was, tied up in his own kitchen while she strolled through the other three rooms like someone about to become the new tenant. He could hear her opening and closing doors, slamming drawers, and rattling bottles in his medicine cabinet. Finally, she came back to the kitchen.

"Before I start tearing the place apart, how about something to eat?" She opened the refrigerator door and began pushing jars. Foster could not see what she was doing, but he could almost identify the various containers by their clinks—pickles, mustard, ketchup.

"Christ, what do you live on?"

"My nephew brings me groceries. He's supposed to deliver some today." McGee knew how weak the line sounded, like a little boy telling another kid, 'You'd better be nice to me 'cause my daddy will be home soon, and he'll beat you up."

"Yeah, right. I hope he does come. Maybe he'll bring us some steak and lobster tails." She slammed the Kelvinator door and went to the cabinets. After a couple of incorrect guesses, she found a jar of peanut butter and a box of saltines. Foster watched her take a saucer and knife from the drain board before she sat at the table, facing him, smearing the crackers and watching him.

"You know, you're pretty neat for an old fart. Are you queer, or something? I mean, if my old man lived alone, the place would be a pigsty. So are you?"

"What?"

"Queer! I just said that."

Foster could feel his face flush. He didn't know girls talked like that. "No, I'm not queer. I just have trouble with ants."

She nodded in understanding as if the two of them were old friends sharing home remedies to rid their houses of pests. She didn't say any more, and when she finished eating, she rinsed the knife and brushed the crumbs from the table.

"Okay, old guy, where do you keep it?" She wiped her damp hands on her jeans, and now Foster watched her standing, arms crossed, in front of him. Now she was going to kill him; he was certain. She hadn't cleaned up her mess to be polite. She was covering her tracks. Destroying evidence.

"You mean money?"

The girl kicked Foster's ankle, sending a shock up his spine. "Now what the hell do you think I mean?"

"I don't have much."

"Yeah, yeah. Cut the crap. Where is it?" He could hear the impatience in her voice, but something instinctively told him not to give it all up, to keep her needing more, to keep her needing him.

"In the cabinet." He signaled with his head. "In the baking powder can."

The girl threw open the cabinet door and rummaged through a hoard of ancient spices until she pulled out the Calumet can from the back. She giggled like a child when she opened the lid and pulled out a bundle of bills bound with a rubber band. "I guess this helps your dough rise, huh?"

Foster did not smile. He held his breath. He knew her excitement was going to fade any minute when she actually counted the cash from the cache. He only kept enough money stashed there to pay the paperboy or to buy stamps from the rural mail carrier.

The girl tried to straighten the bills on the table, but they continued to roll back into themselves. Finally, she finished counting.

"Thirteen goddamned dollars!"

She scraped her chair back from the table and stomped toward him. Foster closed his eyes and waited for the blow of her fist. Instead, he felt a pressure on his lap. She had straddled him on the chair, and now her face was within inches of his. The vee of her legs pressed just below his waist.

"Let's try again. Where do you keep your money?" She said the words very slowly as if he were a child or someone who did not speak fluent English.

Foster could feel the heat from her body, her crotch against him, and he was filled with embarrassment, fear, desire. He'd never known these emotions were so closely related. What did she plan to do to him? Before he could turn his head away, she grabbed his ears and crushed her mouth onto his, forcing open his lips and jabbing her tongue inside until he made a muffled sound of surrender. At that moment he recalled a stone he'd carved many years before. It was for a young girl who'd been raped, murdered, and left in a field to rot. At the time, he'd wondered about her terror at the moment she'd died, and he'd doubted that his relief-carved angel could comfort such a soul. Now he knew he'd been right.

"Liked that, didn't you, you old coot?" The girl stood up and folded her arms, strong and well formed, across her chest. "Still not going to tell me, are you? Too bad."

She entered the kitchen, flinging pots and pans, lids skittering across the floor. Next, she moved to the bathroom. He could hear the breakage of glass and the bounce of plastic containers in the porcelain sink.

"Two down and two to go," she announced as she went into the parlor, separated from the kitchen by two rough beams that went from ceiling to floor.

Foster could see her digging through the papers and magazines behind the stove. "What is this? You from Arizona or something?" She had grabbed a stack of *Arizona Highways* and was fanning them out around her on the floor.

"No."

"Then why all the magazines?"

"I like the pictures."

"And . . . ." The girl obviously wasn't satisfied with his answer.

"I like to imagine I'm there instead of here."

Foster watched her as she lay on her stomach, propped her chin in her hand, and opened to the glossy pictures as if she were any normal teenager looking through a movie magazine.

"Wow, this is beautiful."

She brought a recent volume over for him to see. He recognized the photograph.

"That's Flagstaff. Sometimes it snows there in the summer . . . in the mountains."

She returned to her seat and continued to look through the stack until she finally remembered what she was looking for. "Shit," she murmured to herself when she glanced at the clock on the wall. She pushed the magazines away, stood up, and headed for the closet.

The old man wanted to cry out that there was nothing valuable inside, but he knew if he did, she'd be suspicious and open the boxes. Maybe, just maybe, she wouldn't bother opening them all if he sat quietly. But even as he thought this, he knew it wasn't possible. She would open the door, sift through the newspaper, and find all he had hidden away.

"This looks more like it." She threw him a grin over her shoulder, and for the first time, Foster realized she could be pretty.

Carefully, she removed the first shoebox. At first, she seemed puzzled by the newspaper, but she soon realized there was something inside the wrapping. She tore away at the print until a magnificent swan flew out, its wings spread, and its head tilted upward in a song or a cry. She looked up at Foster but said nothing. Hurriedly, she tore into the next lump of wrapping like a child at a charity Christmas party. They emerged—a mermaid, wave-like hair protecting her modesty; a bearded centaur with prancing hooves and curly fetlocks; a griffin, lion and eagle fused into a flash of fury. On and on.

The old man watched the girl's face as she discovered each new treasure, and he imagined he caught a softening there, much like the expressions he had sometimes noticed on the faces of elderly widows. When ordering stones for their late husbands, they sometimes slipped into the past, and for just a few seconds, he could glimpse the beautiful young brides they had once been. Now this girl became a small child again, positioning the carvings in a semi-circle around her as if they were tea party guests.

"You made all these?" She hadn't opened all the boxes, but the floor was populated with an array of odd creatures, some from mythology, some from Foster's mind alone.

"Yes, damn you." Foster could feel a tear running down his face, and he felt like a fool because he could not wipe it away.

He watched the girl very carefully wrap each figure and return it to its box. Instead of placing the boxes on the closet floor, she removed the unopened ones as well. "Mind if I take these with me?" She wasn't really asking his permission, he knew. "You wouldn't happen to have a car, would you?"

He did not answer. Foster McGee realized that she was getting ready to go, taking with her the only work in his life that he had any right to be proud. If Foster had believed in God, he would have thought this was divine retribution. He tried to remember a Bible passage from childhood about hiding your light under a bushel basket, but all escaped him except his moral.

She would leave. He would stay. Foster felt sure now that she would not kill him. James would come by in a day or two and find him still tied to the chair, if he hadn't died of dehydration by then. Or maybe she would release him before she left. He had no phone or car, and he was too old to follow her on foot. What harm could he do? Everything would be back to normal.

At that moment, Foster experienced a revelation, an epiphany. He did not want everything to be back to normal. He did not want to die alone inside this shack by the side of the highway and have James discover his body a week after the maggots had. This was his only chance. She was his only chance for escape.

"Well, do you have a car or not?"

"Why? Did you steal the one you're driving?"

The girl's head snapped up, and she smiled. "Pretty smart old bastard, huh? Yeah, I took it from my daddy's garage, and I'm sure by now every cop in the country is looking for it."

Foster held her eyes for a moment. "I don't have a car, but I think I can help."

He could see her eyes narrow. She thought he was trying to trick her, he could tell. Maybe he was in a way. "Now why in the hell would you want to help me?"

"Maybe we can help each other. If you untie me, I'll show you."

He could see the girl's mind churning, could almost watch her calculating the time it would take a bullet to pierce his brain. At last, she walked behind him and untied the knot. He could feel the blood creep back into fingers, and his arms felt stiff and heavy.

"Okay, Gramps, what can you do to help me?"

"You only need three things." He shuffled over to a drawer in the kitchen and pulled out the stack of unused bumper stickers that he'd salvaged from Nell's throwaway heap. James always picked them up on their trips, and Nell always refused to let him deface the bumper of their Oldsmobile. Now, they could be useful.

"We'll put these all over the back of the car."

She smiled. "You're a natural born car thief, I can tell. What's the second thing I need?"

"Outside."

She followed him out the door they'd entered hours before. It was still light outside, but the sky was growing dusky. Foster stopped and looked back at the front wall. Somewhere he'd tacked what he was looking for. There. The middle petal of the second daisy. A current Arizona license plate that had skidded off the highway a couple weeks ago. He dug his fingernails behind the metal, pulled it free, and handed it to the girl.

"Okay, that's number two. What's left?"

Foster straightened his shoulders. He didn't know what her reaction might be—a blow to the temple with gun, a quick kick to the groin. "I'm number three."

"What do you mean?"

Foster felt his courage soar. She was confused, not furious. "I want to go with you. I can drive. They're going to be looking for a young girl behind the wheel, not an old man."

She started shaking her head, but Foster could tell it wasn't a negative response to his suggestion, only disbelief. "You want to come with me? Why? I just robbed you, for Christ's sake."

The only way Foster McGee could explain was to simply hold out his hand and sweep it around them, asking her to take it all in, to see that he had nothing here to give up.

The girl let the gun drop. "Okay, but I'm only giving you five minutes to grab a few clothes. I don't want a smelly old goat in the car with me."

Foster shuffled inside. He threw a few pieces of clothing into a canvas bag he'd bought for a hospital trip a couple years before, making sure to take the pair of green socks, rolled together in a ball. These were the ones that held his money, the cash the girl couldn't find. When he came out of the bedroom, he saw that she had removed the bundled carvings from their boxes and stuffed them inside grocery bags with handles.

"Help me carry all this stuff." She didn't wait to see if he followed.

Foster scooped up the remaining bags. On the way out, he didn't worry about shutting the door. One way or another, he wouldn't be coming back here.

"By the way, where are we going?" he called out to the girl's back.

She paused to put the sacks over the fence before crawling through. "Look at the license plate. We're just a girl and her grandpa on our way home to Arizona."

Foster could feel a trembling inside. He knew he couldn't trust the girl, like a wolf cub raised in captivity but savage by instinct. Still, she needed him to get to Arizona. And if, once there, she kicked him from the car, he'd find his way to the desert alone. Saguaros were waiting. He'd read about the cacti that waited all year only to bloom for one day. Only one. But that would be enough.

A fiction writer and poet, Linda Neal Reising is a native of Oklahoma and a member of the Western Cherokee Nation. She has taught English for over thirty years and just completed her twenty-seventh year at North Posey Jr. High School, where she teaches eighth grade. Linda has been published in the *Southern Indiana Review*, the *Comstock Review*, and *Open 24 Hours*. Her work has been included in *Fruitflesh: Seeds of Inspiration for Women Who Write*, a book published by HarperCollins. Linda also has poetry forthcoming in *And Know This Place*, an anthology of Indiana poets writing about Indiana. Judges recently named her the first place winner of the Judith Siegel Pearson Writing Award, a national competition for a collection of poetry concerning women.

The Prize

J. Myers Birsner

My dad raised my brother and me on stories about growing up in Logan and Lincoln counties in Oklahoma. As the main character of these stories, he seemed daring and strange. He was so independent, even in his teens, self-sufficient and enterprising, not the same person who went to work every day, mowed the lawn, carried the family to church, and never took a vacation.

The youth he described was unpredictable and full of adventures that we, in our conventional and regular lives, found unreal. We often responded with disbelief.

"Really, Dad? That really happened?" He swore the stories were true, but we enjoyed them only as something he told to entertain us. They were just too exciting, too innovative to believe. Often people who knew Dad urged him to write about his life. He had been orphaned, carried away from his home, lived through the Great Depression and the World Wars, and built several businesses.

His life had been exceptional and worth recording, and his stories were, in fact, true. He helped me write some of these stories; we spent time looking at old newspapers and town histories that confirmed what he had told us over the years. This story about the Bunion Derby is one of those.

jmb

The Prize

"Betty, I want to show you something." I drew my sister to the kitchen table and placed the November 23, 1927 issue of the *Tulsa World* in front of her. "Look at that. Read it." I pointed to a bold headline that stood out among the columns of the sports section, "Race Calls for Entrants."

"What is it?" Betty asked. She sat down and began to read.

I watched her eyes go from line to line. How many times did she go over it? It was hard for me to keep quiet. Since I first read about C. C. Pyle's cross-country foot race from Los Angeles to New York City, I could think of nothing else. Now I had to ask my guardian for her approval. My sister Betty was twenty-seven. She had taken care of me since our mother died when I was a baby.

She looked up from the paper at last and said, "That's something, isn't it?"

"I'm gonna enter," I burst out.

"You? You're too young."

I shook my head and tried to sound reasonable, "No I'm not. There's no limit on age. Anyone can enter."

"She stood up and the legs of the wooden chair scraped on the old linoleum floor. "Well, you're not, Hal. You've got to finish high school. Why, that would take—how long would it take? I can't imagine."

I stepped directly in front of her, looked her in the eye. "I know I can do it. I'm strong and I can train. And the money! First prize twenty-five thousand dollars! And if I don't come in first, the next four get big money too!"

She looked at me without saying anything for several moments. "You can't leave home now. You have to finish school, get a good job, and—"

I stopped her before she said no again, "Don't answer now. Just think about it, will you?"

Eyes that rarely smiled gave me a look I could read well, a look that said give it up, get on with important things like taking care of dinner and the dishes and finishing your homework and getting yourself to bed so you can get up and hit it all again in the morning—early.

Betty had to quit high school when she was fifteen to help raise younger brothers and sisters. Pop brought the boys, my three brothers and me, from Ohio to Oklahoma in 1918, and the four girls came out as they each finished high school. I was the youngest boy, and Pop died when I was seven. We kids scattered among aunts, uncles, and cousins. Betty took my brother Joe and me to live with her in Chandler. She had been married only six months.

"Go on and see to Stan," I said. "I'll finish cleaning up." I folded the newspaper between my schoolbooks and began putting the plates and silverware from supper into the sink. Betty walked out of the kitchen. I could hear her talking to her one-year-old as she dressed him for bed. In a moment she came back to mix a tablespoon of honey and lemon juice in hopes that she could get him to sleep without the asthmatic cough that could keep us awake all night. She didn't say anything more.

The next morning my alarm went off one hour early, four a.m. I put on as many clothes as I could: warmth for the late autumn temperatures, weight to make the work-out as strenuous as possible, and heavy lace-up shoes. I did a few stretches and jumps in the dark front yard and headed down our dirt road away from town. My training had begun.

For weeks, I ran the miles of country roads around Chandler. Each day I got up a few minutes earlier and added more and more distance. My dreams had always been running, down a football field or a basketball court, always toward the goal at the end of the run. Now I could see myself breaking the tape in New York City, being borne on the shoulders of the jubilant crowd. I had thrown the long pass, knocked in the winning run, and sunk the final goal, all the heroic efforts that won the contest. I had known victory, and I would know it again—and grow rich at the same time. Running wasn't work. It was joy.

My plan was to increase my distance to fifty miles a day for the race. It would require at least that to cover the 3,400 miles across the country, and I would have to quit school and train to do it. I worked up to six or seven miles before the sun rose. I had a long way to go and had to commit right away, or I wouldn't be ready for the starting gun in Los Angeles on March 4, 1928, two weeks before my sixteenth birthday.

There were two requirements I had to meet to enter the race, now called by the newspapers the Bunion Derby. First, was an entry fee of a hundred dollars, and second was enough money to cover my meals and expenses during the race.

I had to talk to Betty again, get her answer. But before I did, I wanted to be able to tell her that I had raised the necessary money for myself, assure her that it wouldn't cost her anything. She didn't have it, and she would worry about me being broke so far away from home.

I had worked since I was ten years old. Any odd job that I could scare up I was willing to do, throwing papers, making deliveries, sweeping and cleaning nearly every business in town. Because of this, I knew many merchants in Chandler, and these were my potential sponsors. Mr. Stoltenberger, owner of the grocery and market on Manvel Street, was interested and encouraging. He promised to help with my expenses. And Mr. Hereford, who ran the dry goods store, said he would make up what I lacked for the entry fee.

I also had a good friend in the town barber, Gilbert Waggoner, who was caught up in my adventure.

"You can do it Hal. You're just mean enough to tough it out."

I sat in his barber chair, and he faced me, sitting on a stool. "I've already started training."

"Tell me how the race works. I know you have to run so many miles a day. Who keeps track?"

"There'll be check-in stations set up along Highway 66 where everyone spends the night. Each runner has until midnight to get to the station and have his time recorded. Then at the end of the race, the one with the shortest time for the whole distance is the winner. And every day the distance is different, anywhere from twenty to sixty miles. It depends on how far apart the stations are. But you run at your own pace, stop to eat or whatever. It's up to you. You just have to get to each station by midnight."

Gilbert was thoughtful. "I heard someone else from Oklahoma's gonna enter too, a guy from Claremore." I had just gotten this bit of news. Gilbert could hardly sit still. "Does that scare you?"

"Nah, I heard about him. Besides, there's gonna be people from everywhere. They're even coming from foreign countries."

"What about this Oklahoma guy?"

"The papers say he ran track in high school. A farm boy, one of seven children and the town is helping him raise money to enter."

"Well, you've got as much of a chance as he does."

"That's what I figure."

"You've got your entry money promised already, haven't you?" he asked. I nodded. "I've been doing some thinking, Hal. You're gonna need someone with you, someone to take care of your gear and meals. I'm a single man with no ties. I'd be willing to go." He paused a moment. "Hell, maybe I could pick up some bucks for myself along the way. People are gonna need haircuts even on a cross country marathon. Right?"

"Right!" I sat there grinning.

"You got a car lined up?" he asked.

He had done some thinking, and in detail. "No, I haven't got that far yet."

"Don't worry about it. We can take my pick-up." He laughed aloud, "This is gonna be great! We'll be famous!"

He turned to the mirror behind the barber chair and began grooming his own hair, humming as he combed. He was a dapper looking guy, and excitement glowed in his eyes.

"What about this guy from Oklahoma? Can we find out more about the local competition?"

"I heard he's running in plowed fields to toughen his feet. Sounds like he's serious, doesn't it?" We were silent for a moment. "Well, I gotta go, Gil. I'll get back with you after I talk to Betty." At the door I turned, "Thanks."

I waited several evenings for the proper moment to speak to her. Her husband Edward worked nights at the power plant, so we were often alone after supper. She was usually tired from work herself, and moody, but finally the time seemed to be right. My homework and chores were done, and Stanley had gone to sleep without much trouble. Since I first brought up the subject of the race I had dropped many hints, but Betty had never mentioned it. I tried to anticipate every possible objection my sister might have—money, school, work, everything—and rehearsed my speech over and over again in my head. She was hard to convince once she'd made up her mind, and I sensed she had on this issue.

"I've worked out some things I want to tell you. About the race," I said.

She began to shake her head.

"Let me talk a minute. I've worked things out. You don't have to worry about anything." I took a deep breath. "First of all, I would miss only one semester of school. I would train beginning right now 'til the race starts in March. The race will take three or four months through the summer, and I would be back in school next fall." I paused to gauge her expression. Her face had clouded over, but she didn't say anything.

"I've got people to help with my expenses, business people from town, so it won't cost us anything. And—"

"You've talked to other people about this?" She asked.

"Yes, that's the way these things are done. You have to get sponsors. I've even got someone to go with me so I won't be alone. Gilbert Waggoner's gonna take his truck and carry my food and stuff."

She stood up, "Don't talk to anyone else, Hal. You can't go."

"Why not?" I exploded. "You have no reason! I've worked everything out."

Her voice fired back, "If you leave school, you'll never finish. It is too hard. Every one of us has had to fight and work to get through high school. It took me 'til I was twenty. You're the last one of us, and you're not going to go through that too."

"I promise I will, Betty. I'll finish high school because I want to go to college. That's the reason I'm doing this. Without the money, I could never make it. You know that. It's hard enough now getting through high school and doing all the extra jobs I can. This is a great chance, and I think I can do it. Maybe not first place."

She began to pace around the room and brushed a strand of hair off her forehead. He face looked drawn. "You're too young. California's too far and Gilbert's just a kid himself. No telling what he'd get you into. I'd worry myself sick."

I fought to keep my voice level. "Betty, I'll be running forty, fifty miles a day. I'll be too beat to get into trouble. This is big time, serious stuff." I paused and took a breath. "If I win, I'll have everything. College. A place to live. I can take care of myself. You won't have to." I ran out of things to say, and Betty wouldn't look at me.

"You can't go, Hal," she said firmly and quietly. Her eyes filled with tears. We both stood as though frozen in place. I couldn't get a breath past my throat, and Betty had her back to me by this time.

I could never remember my sister crying, even when Pop died. She was made of iron. I had always needed Betty because of my youth, because there was no one else. I had never thought she might need me. I remembered what she had gone through when Stan was born. The doctor didn't come for hours. Edward wasn't home. I thought she might die. But she was a fighter, and we fought through it together. She never let go of my hand, calling first for Mama and then for me.

Right then I realized that the decision to enter the race was mine to make. I could go even if Betty didn't want me to. But I knew I wouldn't. I would stay. Betty was the only parent I had ever had, and I wasn't ready to tell her goodbye.

Thanksgiving and Christmas holidays were strained, not the usual happy feasts and presents. I just didn't have anything to say. I spent my time away from the house as much as possible, nursing my disappointments, my training now focused on shooting free throws and maintaining my stamina for the end of basketball season. My routine of school, sports, and odd jobs continued. Every morning after I delivered the *Tulsa World*, I settled down with the sports page. I had always been a sports nut and could not help but follow the particulars of the Bunion Derby even though I was in Chandler instead of California. Caught up in the daily momentum of the race, I began to let go of the pain of not being included. The race was regular news, and when it began in March, with only one runner from Oklahoma, there were 276 entrants.

Favorites in the race were known names in the world of long distance running. Arthur Newton from Rhodesia, South Africa, had won many one-hundred-mile races. Ed Gardner, a Negro athlete from Seattle, was expected to do well, and the champion Canadian walker, Phillip Granville, had entered. Runners from Finland, Italy, England, and all over our own country were in the marathon. The Oklahoma farm boy, Andrew

Payne, was among the youngest entrants at nineteen. The oldest was Charles Hart from England, aged sixty-three. My buddy, Gil Waggoner and I kept up with the race, daily predicting who would come in the winner. Gil was excited when we plotted to enter, and he never lost enthusiasm even as we experienced the race from a distance.

Spring practice began for the high school football team when the Bunion Derby had been going on for two weeks. The number of runners had decreased to fewer than one hundred. I read about the terrible punishment from blisters and torn muscles and an epidemic of tonsillitis that eliminated many contestants. It had become a race of endurance. Things weren't much different at home. I often felt like an itinerant worker there, but for the first time Betty and Edward began to keep up with my own sports schedule and even requested updates on the progress of the Bunion Derby.

On March 20, 1928, Andy Payne replaced the frontrunner, forty-four year-old Arthur Newton, who dropped from the race because of a sprained ankle. The runners were approaching the Arizona–New Mexico border along U.S. Highway 66. Payne's first place was threatened daily by the black runner Gardner and Peter Gavuzzi of Southampton, England.

The group was to run across Oklahoma, and Chandler had been designated an overnight station. Runners were scheduled to arrive April 14th.

I delivered flyers throughout Lincoln County urging Saturday shoppers to come early and witness the one-of-a-kind sporting event that brought people from across the world to Chandler, Oklahoma. Our town planned a huge welcome for the runners and the extensive caravan that accompanied them, described by the *Lincoln County Republican* as an "almost complete town on wheels." There were 115 vehicles of all sizes and descriptions that traveled with the racers as well as sideshows, hospital, radio station, café, hotel, and nearly five-hundred people to serve the delegation.

Red Grange was a part of the entourage along with the sponsor of the marathon, C. C. Pyle. They were traveling across the country just ahead of the runners to promote the event and arrange accommodations at the overnight stops.

On the day of their arrival, the high school letter club met in town as part of the host committee. We wore our maroon sweaters with blue chenille Cs proclaiming us members of the athletic teams. I wanted to meet Red Grange.

The weather was cloudy and blustery, but it was a great day. Chandler had been taken over by thousands of spectators and followers of the race. Vehicles lined the main street all the way out of town along the highway to wait, and about noon, the advance caravan rolled in, led by three huge buses. I joined the crowds that filled the street and swarmed through the swirling dust to meet the buses parked in the middle of Manvel.

The first bus was painted pale yellow, a rolling lounge like a railroad Pullman car, plush and comfortable. I knew this was for the celebrities and held my breath when the door opened. Out stepped the most magnificent human being I had ever seen. He was about six-foot-four, slender, and had vibrant red hair lifted and tossed by the wind. He was immaculate in knife-pleat navy slacks and dress shirt open at the collar.

Immediately he moved into the crowd, shaking hands and thanking everyone for coming out to meet the runners. I was so enthralled just watching him that my feet wouldn't move. I didn't feel the motion of those around me who crowded forward to meet and touch Red Grange. Then he slipped out of my sight, and it was too late to catch up.

A smaller man who looked like a high-powered businessman in a pin-striped suit got off the bus behind Red. It was Charlie Pyle, promoter of the cross-country race. In contrast to Grange, he was quiet and self-effacing and sought out the community fathers to receive their welcome. He announced that the runners would begin arriving toward the middle of the afternoon.

The weather didn't improve, and at two-thirty, it was still cloudy and miserable. Highway 66, called by the *Lincoln County Republican* "The Main Street of America," was a one-lane dirt road that became the brick paved Manvel Street of Chandler. Spectators stood at the end of the hard surface and down the rough road in thick blowing dust to watch for the runners. They were coming fifty-two miles from Oklahoma City.

Finally, out of the dirty red clouds we saw a figure loping toward town. My heart pounded. Gil and I elbowed our way to the front of the crowd. At last, I would lay eyes on the famous Andy Payne.

But as the runner came closer, his form didn't fit the description I knew of a sinewy racer dressed in bright white track shirt and shorts. This was something altogether different, unexpected. I squinted in the gritty air to get a better look. Into the town, into the twentieth century came something out of an exotic fantasy—a dark figure wearing a burnoose, flapping in the Oklahoma wind, the hood drawn over his head and across the lower part of his face. The only parts of his body we could see were his legs, spindly and short, churning through the blowing red dirt and onto the cobblestones of the town. People around me roared in greeting and opened a path for him to pass, and he pumped on toward the courthouse in the square. I learned later that it was an athlete from Trieste.

The next runner appeared in about thirty minutes, and he too was shrouded in protective clothing, though not as bizarre as the Italian racer we had just seen. It was Peter Gavuzzi who had been running along with Payne for most of the race and was in second place in total elapsed time.

Runners straggled in irregularly, and I saw that the Negro community had assembled to greet Ed Gardner, now running in sixth place. Mrs. Shawner, superintendent of the colored school, drove her big Lincoln, and when Gardner arrived, she and the welcoming group joyfully gathered him into their midst and carried him off to a private celebration.

Along with the racers appeared an interesting variety of vehicles that carried their personal companions and helpers. Anything from rattletrap pick-up trucks and motorcycles to long low sedans drove unevenly into town, shadowing the runners.

But although the accompanying vehicles were different, I noticed a particular sameness about the contestants. Their bodies were taut, hard muscled, and when they got to their stopping place for the night, it was difficult for them to get out of the frantic rhythm of running. They walked around as I had seen horses do after a race, to slow and cool their bodies, to return their breathing to a normal rate.

Many of them were in pain, either from injuries to their limbs or emotional pressure from within. Their faces were weathered, strained. They searched with eyes that were lonely and old for the faces of their trainers and gladly fell under their ministrations. I calculated that they had run less than half the race, and I pitied them. That day in Chandler three more quit the race, unable to endure the daily pace or confront the remaining two thousand miles to New York City.

It was nearly four o'clock before the leader of the race arrived, and we showed our appreciation in cheers loud and long. Payne's attire was characteristic; he stood out in his traditional track uniform with only a light jacket against the chill wind. Andy's skin was leather-like, and he wore a stoic, determined expression. But he smiled at our reception and waved to us. I read earlier in the week that being back on Oklahoma soil had given him a lift, and this was revealed in his face in contrast to the faces of the many weary runners who plodded into town and looked only for quick and quiet rest.

Andy's father and other family members joined him, escorting him to the Egbert Hotel for the night. The remainder of the evening was festive. There were dinners and parties everywhere, and I was caught up in the celebration. The high school had been opened to runners and trainers who needed a place to stay. The hotels and restaurants were full. This night there was no curfew, and I prowled the streets trying to locate and observe anyone interesting. In particular, I wanted to catch up with Red Grange. However, the guests retired early and enjoyed a private meal and room while my friends and I experienced the excitement of knowing they were somewhere near. Until midnight, the periodic announcement of the mobile radio station noted the arrival of each racer.

I had to satisfy myself with the thought of getting up early the next morning, even though it was Sunday, and seeing the caravan on its way. I wouldn't be denied then. I was bringing my football, and I would shake The Red's hand.

The spring sky was hazy at seven in the morning, when people started gathering in the middle of town to send the caravan and runners on their way to Bristow and Tulsa and parts northeast. I had been up since five delivering papers and then staking out a place between the Egbert Hotel and the lead bus to spot the celebrity and have him autograph my football.

I knew all about Red Grange, called by sports writers The Galloping Ghost. He had recently graduated from the University of Illinois and became involved in the formation of a professional football league with C. C. Pyle. He was known for his running abilities and sure instinct for the goal line. I often tried to emulate his tactics as tailback in the single wing formation on our Chandler team. From newspaper reviews and radio broadcasts of his games, I envisioned just how he would operate on the field. By seeing and talking to him in person, maybe I would absorb some of his athletic magic. I had missed the Bunion Derby, but a football scholarship could get me through college just as well.

There was a stir among the crowd, and Grange appeared looking rested and fresh. He brought a glow to the morning, an enthusiasm that spread among us all. I worked my way through the crowd to the redhead and held my ball out to him. He grinned.

Up close, his perfections were dazzling. He was shiny and sharp. His eyes, clear and gleaming, reflected purity and goodness. I forgot about the autograph and asked impulsively, "Throw me a pass, Red?"

He looked me over, my letter sweater, my hair parted and slicked to one side, and took the ball from my hands.

In 1928, footballs were somewhat round in shape, thicker than the slender, elongated balls used today. They were also four to six ounces heavier than the modern fourteen-ounce balls. More than a handful.

"Okay, kid, take off," he ordered and pointed down the street.

I took off. I ran halfway down the block to the alley that intersected Manvel, turned, and set myself to receive the pass. But he motioned me to keep going. I ran about twenty yards further and looked back. Again, he waved me on, and I pedaled backwards until I reached the corner.

A block away, I saw Red step apart from the crowd. I set myself a little forward on my feet, expecting to have to run up to catch the pass. Grange was not famous for his passing, although he did throw the ball; his running had gained him his reputation. Nobody could throw a football a whole city block, the entire distance of a football field.

Red rotated the ball in his hands, seeking the laces, and gripped it toward one pointed end. He made a couple of throwing motions to warm up, then eyeballed me. He rocked back, stretched his right arm up behind him, and threw. The ball sailed high and strong, and it was coming fast. I didn't have time to run forward, nor did I need to. I prayed I could catch the ball that homed in to the exact spot where I waited.

I held my hands at waist level, relaxed and ready. The ball came into my midsection and kept going with me wrapped around it. I found myself sitting on my rear end in the middle of Manvel Street, but I came up with the ball. The cheers from the crowd were as sweet to me as if I'd scored the winning touchdown in the conference playoffs.

I trotted back to the bus, its motor rumbling, with a broad smile on my face. Someone patted me on the back, and I saw it was Edward, taking a detour through town on his way home from work. Then it was time for Red to leave. He waved to me and the rest of the town and boarded the bus.

I never felt any regrets at not being a part of the Bunion Derby. After seeing the runners and their poor condition, I counted myself better off for having missed it. Many doctors predicted that the runners had shortened their lives by the terrible strain on their hearts. They continued their odyssey of endurance and pain for over forty days, and only fifty-five runners made it to New York City to the finish line on May 26, 1928. Andy Payne, the boy from Oklahoma, friend of Will Rogers, won the race. His father said he was too stubborn not to finish, and we believed he could because we wanted him to. With the prize money, he paid off his family's mortgage and saw to it that all his brothers and sisters got a high school education.

I had two more years of high school, instead of two and a half, and I had met Red Grange.

A native Oklahoman, Janeen Myers earned her Bachelor's degree in English from Oklahoma State University. She took a long hiatus from education to raise a family and take an active part in her family's business. She began teaching English as a graduate TA at the University of Central Oklahoma where she earned her Master of Arts degree in English studies in 1988. From 1988 through 1993, she taught Freshman Composition classes as an adjunct at UCO, Rose State College, and Oklahoma City Community College.

In 1993, Janeen took a position at Oklahoma State University in Oklahoma City as an English Specialist in the newly organized Learning Center.

At OSU–OKC she taught Composition courses and helped develop and teach freshman orientation courses (Student Success Strategies), which introduced students to online learning. She co-chaired the Writing Across the Curriculum program, attending and presenting at several national conferences. In 1996, she was appointed co-chair of the Honors Program and saw the campus-wide program grow from participation of only a few students to nearly one hundred. In the time since 1996, the Honors Program established Honors courses in English and film, scholarship and cash awards for academic research projects, and student attendance to Honors conferences locally and across the country. After ten years of fulltime teaching, Janeen retired from OSU–OKC.

Making Meaning: Strategies for College Reading, a text for low-reading-level students, was published in 2007. Janeen was lead author, developed the instructor manual, and co-wrote online material to supplement the text. Currently, she writes short fiction for submission to various publishing venues and teaches Freshman Composition at UCO.

www.ingramcontent.com/pod-product-compliance
Lightning Source LLC
LaVergne TN
LVHW011708060526
838200LV00051B/2813